HER DIRTY BODYGUARDS: A FORBIDDEN LOVE ROMANCE

A MEN AT WORK REVERSE HAREM NOVEL

MIKA LANE

HEADLANDS PUBLISHING

GET A FREE SHORT STORY!

Get a free short story!
Join my Insider Group
Exclusive access to private release specials, giveaways, the opportunity to receive advance reader copies (ARCs), and other random musings.

Let's keep in touch
Mika Lane Newsletter
Email me
Visit me! www.mikalane.com
Friend me! Facebook
Pin me! Pinterest
Follow me! Twitter
Laugh with me! Instagram

CHAPTER 1

Lillian 'Lill' Harlowe

"You come very highly recommended."
I smiled humbly.
"Tell me, have you cleaned for many other families?"

"Oh yes. So many," I lied enthusiastically.

Was she kidding? I didn't even clean my own apartment. And it wasn't a fraction of the size of this sprawling Upper East Side two-story apartment I was standing in.

You know how rare two-story apartments are in Manhattan? my BFF Beebie had asked when trying to sell me on the cleaning job.

No, I didn't know. And I didn't care. I wouldn't have

wanted to clean someone's home if it were painted in fucking gold.

Which Amalia von Malsen's home very well could be. I hadn't gotten past the foyer yet.

"Ah, here he is," my new employer said, her polite, nice-to-meet-you smile morphing into something different as she tilted her head demurely and bit her lower lip.

I looked up to find a tall man, gorgeous, of course, because what else would they have in this home, heading toward me, his dress shoes clicking on the marble floor and his sport jacket flying behind him.

Had god ever made a better-looking couple?

She looked up at him adoringly as he approached.

"Apologies for being late, ma'am," he said to her.

Was that how he talked to his wife?

Ew.

And what was that lump under the right side of his jacket? People didn't carry pagers anymore did they?

Unless he was a drug dealer?

"Lillian, this is our head of family security, Callum Deverall," she purred as if she'd designed the man herself.

Oh. Not a husband. A worker bee.

Like me.

And um, that pager? Probably a gun.

"Hello, Lillian," he said, looking me up and down with his impossibly chiseled jawline.

As he sized me up, I was wishing I'd worn something nicer than my H&M skinny jeans and Converse Chucks. By contrast, Amalia looked like she'd floated out of the pages of *Harper's Bazaar*. But I guess that's how you dressed when you didn't have to clean your own home.

He took another step closer to me. "I hope you don't mind, but we need to pat you down before you can enter the von Malsen home any further."

Nobody told me about this part.

I tried to casually laugh, but it came out more like a choking sound. "You're not serious, are you?"

Amalia's smiled faltered, her face growing dark. But only for a moment. She was clearly practiced at 'looking pleasant.' "Lillian, we *are* serious. Everyone new to our staff undergoes a background check and gets patted down for weapons and god knows what *else*" —she gazed up at Mister Security again— "the first time they arrive for work, and then randomly afterward."

Jesus. What had I wandered into? I knew from Beebie, who'd decorated their apartment, that Amalia's husband, the esteemed Eckhart von Malsen, was some kind of important United Nations diplomat. But was patting down the cleaning lady really necessary?

I decided not to make a joke about it being a good thing I'd left my own gun at home.

But Mister Security was freaking hot, and I hadn't been touched by a man in a while. So I caved.

I smiled to show what a pleasant person I was.

"Okay. Um, do we go into another room or something?" I asked, looking between the two of them.

Would he ask me to take my clothes off? That might not be so bad...

Amalia looked at me with scorn. "No, dear. Just put your hands up on the wall right there, and let Cal do his job. And mind the wallpaper."

Holy crap. Just like in the movies.

"I'm not really comfortable with this, Mrs. von Malsen—"

"No," she cried, "please call me Amalia."

Not the point, but okay.

"Amalia—"

She pressed her lips together and sniffed, clearly not used to being questioned. "Lillian, please let Cal do his job so we can all go on about our day."

I looked at Mister Security, hoping for some solidarity. We were both just staff bitches. But the expression on his face didn't indicate he felt the same way.

He gestured toward the wall with his chin, his lips pressed together sternly.

Holy shit. What an ass.

So I turned around and slapped my hands on Amalia's wallpaper, stepping my feet apart, just like they did on TV. And as he moved closer, I bent and pushed my ass out, hoping to 'innocently' graze him.

But he was too fast for me.

He smoothed his hands over my hair, then my shoulders and down my back. He ran his hands over each of my arms and then my legs, squeezing lightly, then around my abdomen and just up to my underwire bra.

Guess they don't feel the boobs.

His hands skimmed my butt cheeks, and then he stopped.

"Is that it?" I asked, trying to see him over my shoulder.

"Yes," he said. "Thank you."

Well. That was kind of lame, as pat-downs go.

Regaining my dignity, I whipped around, I guess a little too fast for Security, because I found my nose inches from his chest.

"Oh. Excuse me," I said, stepping to the side.

Security nodded at Amalia, then click-clicked down the hall to wherever he'd come from.

"Thanks, Cal," Amalia called after him in a dreamy voice.

He turned and nodded. "You're welcome, ma'am."

Suck up.

The smile on her face faded as she turned to me. "Let's go to the kitchen."

Welcome to the von Malsens'.

We passed through a sprawling living room with multiple seating areas reminiscent of a hotel lobby and lots of cool, oversized paintings on the walls.

Damn. Beebie had done an amazing job putting this place together. Guess that's why she was one of New York's top decorators.

"Your home is lovely, Amalia."

She stopped so abruptly I almost plowed into her. "It's the view that sold us," she announced, gesturing toward French doors that opened onto a terrace, and city skyline beyond.

I could see why.

New York was a crazy place to be with its endless noise, smells, and throngs of different sorts of humanity. But a sanctuary like this would make for a whole different experience, especially compared to what I was used to. My apartment building had a permanent slight garbage-y smell, which no amount of Lysol could cover up. The hallways were strewn like a minefield with bicycles and baby carriages people couldn't fit into their tiny apartments. And our views looked straight into the apartments across the alley, including that of one chubby guy who liked to clean naked.

Coming home to this sort of Upper East Side hermetically-sealed perfection, where the only smell was of the roses on the dining table and the only sounds were of classical music playing in a distant room, would wash away any discomforts the Big Apple might throw one's way.

I could live in one of these vertical mansions, no problem.

That's what Beebie called them, *vertical mansions*.

"Have a seat," Amalia said, gesturing to a stool at the counter.

The kitchen was no less impressive than anything

else I'd seen so far, naturally, with its all white tile and stainless appliances. "Beebie did a really good job here, too."

She'd told me the white and stainless look was an awful trend that would be tired in five years.

Joke's on you, lady.

Amalia returned from the fridge with two Diet Cokes.

I hated Diet Coke.

"She did. Beebie's so very talented," Amalia said, nodding proudly, like she'd discovered her. "How do you know her?"

"We met in yoga. She's my best friend."

Amalia looked like she'd sucked a lemon. "Oh. I thought you did cleaning for her."

Crap. Was that the story Beebie had told her?

Guess Amalia didn't like that her prestigious and very high-end interior designer had a friend who cleaned houses.

But the truth was, I didn't really clean houses. I was just pretending to clean houses. Temporarily, god willing. I'd just been let go from my crappy job at a daycare center, where they'd somehow intuited I couldn't stand kids.

I had to work on that *being too transparent* thing.

The day care center hadn't been much of a job, but I'd made enough to cover my cheap rent-controlled dump of an apartment, and it left me plenty of time to take classes and write. When I'd griped to Beebie that the job had come to an unceremonious end, she told me one of her clients was just lamenting that her housekeeper had bailed on her, and why didn't I try to fill my job gap with something in a fancy Upper East Side home?

I wasn't sure why she thought cleaning the dirt of a wealthy family was somehow preferable to that of a less well-off family, but I was in no position to be picky. Rent was due in one week, and I'd just spent the small cash cushion I had on an expensive dress for events where I planned to network and meet people.

"I used to clean for Beebie," I corrected myself. "I just don't, um, clean for her now."

Amalia nodded, taking a long draw on her soda. "She also told me you're working on a book or something?"

Beebie had also told me this woman might have industry connections—the most valuable currency in town. Everybody in New York wanted *connections.* They wanted to connect, and be connected to. It was how things worked here, and as soon as I'd caught on to the way the game was played, I began filling my own dance card with all the people I could meet.

It would someday pay off, everybody told me.

And in order to collect these relationships, you had to act the part. Thus, the expensive dress.

My shoes were second-hand, though.

I studied Amalia, wondering how much I could share with her. She'd been snotty as hell in the foyer, but I guess now that she was confident I was not a weapon-carrying criminal, she'd relaxed.

"I'm a writer," I said proudly.

No one would ever know how long I had to practice that in front of the mirror before I could say it with determination.

To be honest, I still wilted a little on the inside when I spoke the words. But I'd like to think I hid it well.

"I have one romance novel under my belt, and another in the works," I added.

Amalia waved her hand, I figured about to add something like 'stick with it,' or 'what a great calling.'

Instead she followed up with a healthy scoff. "A writer? Just like everyone else in New York."

Oh no she didn't.

I felt heat creeping from my neck, where it tiptoed up and onto my face. In moments, there was moisture on my temples, and my mouth was dry as a desert.

I sipped the Diet Coke before I choked. Or choked the woman in front of me.

God, did people love to dump on writers.

Writers don't make any money.

Writers are alcoholics.

Writers are lonely.

The list of what I'd heard over the years could probably fill its own book. The comments came from nearly everyone—my mother, people I barely knew like Amalia, and even fellow students in my writing classes.

Seriously, as if being a writer wasn't hard enough, people are gunning for you to fall on your ass from the get-go.

Fuck that.

Fuck the naysayers.

And fuck Amalia.

Instead of letting her know she'd riled me, I put my hands up like *right?*

"I *love* how there are so many writers here in New York. It's so great for learning and networking, and there are so many opportunities to do interesting work."

Okay, that was kind of bullshitty.

Amalia set her soda down and stood. "Ready to get going?"

CHAPTER 2

Lill

I wasn't kidding when I said I couldn't clean. But, fortunately for me, modern technology was on my side. I ducked into the first of the five bathrooms I was to clean, turned on the tub faucet full-force to hide the noise, and pulled up a YouTube video.

Turned out I wasn't the only person out there wanting to clean a bathroom. After I'd scrubbed the toilet, sink, and bath, I got to work on the tile floor and walls. When I was done, I was quite pleased with the results.

Now I just had to do it four more times. And my back was already hurting.

I had no idea where Amalia had taken off to, but I figured the rest of the bathrooms must be upstairs.

Imagine. An apartment with stairs in it.

I made my way up a curved staircase, laden with my bucket of cleaning supplies, when I looked up and saw Mister Security waiting for me at the top of the steps.

"How's the first day?" he asked.

"Fine," I mumbled, brushing past him.

I poked my head into the first room I came across, looking for another bathroom.

"Need help finding something?"

I turned and gave him my best stink eye. "No," I said in a flat voice, and kept on walking.

First thing the dude had to learn was that *we were not going to be friends*.

No, someone who was dickish enough to feel me up five minutes after I walked in the door didn't deserve any of my time. I don't care if he was the head of the Pope's security. He could fuck himself.

"Lillian! There you are!" Amalia called, rushing toward me.

Cripes. Did I already mess something up?

She'd changed into a form-fitting red dress that stopped mid-thigh. It flattered her minuscule figure perfectly, if you liked women built like twelve-year-olds.

I guess when you had a lot of money, you were able to hang on to your prepubescent shape.

"Lillian, if you don't have plans this evening, could you stay later?"

There was one hot roller in her hair that she'd missed. I didn't tell her.

"I need a sitter for Robbie. The nanny can't come in."

Robbie? Who was Robbie?

She read the confusion on my face. "Robbie is our little boy. And I'll pay you double your hourly rate. It's just until we get back from the fundraiser for his high school."

"He's in high school?"

She looked at me like I was an idiot.

"He's six years old, Lillian. He's in kindergarten. This is for the high school we *want* him to attend in eight years."

They were fundraising for a school that they *hoped* their kid would get into?

I'd definitely stumbled into some sort of alternative universe.

My first thought was to say no. In fact, the words were on the tip of my tongue. As my former employer, the day care center, had figured out, I *did not like kids*.

But I needed the damn money. If I could become a cleaning lady for money, I could babysit for money.

"Um, sure. Okay. What time does he go to bed?"

But she was so pleased she didn't even hear my question. She just bounced a little in her shoes, clapped, and ran off to hopefully get the last curler out of her hair.

I sighed and gathered my cleaning supplies.

Mister Security was still standing there.

"Want me to introduce you to Robbie?" he offered.

Jesus guy. Get the hint.

"No. I can do that myself." I continued down a long corridor, now looking for bathrooms *and* a six-year-old child.

"Boo," a little voice screamed.

And there was the blond, wild-haired rugrat whose high school had already been chosen for him, his hands formed into claws and his face scrunched into a six-year-old's idea of scary.

"You must be Robbie."

Disappointed he hadn't convinced me he was some sort of monster, he dropped his hands.

Then he looked past me and his face lit up. "Hi, Cal!"

His gaze returned to me. "Hey, did you know that Cal has *guns*? Cal, can we see your guns, *please?*" Robbie begged.

Okay. So, the kid liked Mister Security. Then why the hell wasn't *he* the one babysitting?

I might not have guns, but the kid would like me just fine when he realized I'd let him stay up late and eat all the candy he wanted.

I said I'd watch the kid, not be freaking Mary Poppins.

When the bathrooms were done, I hid in the laundry room, looking for another YouTube vid on how to use Amalia's high tech washer and dryer.

My experience with laundry was pretty much limited to the low-tech machines in the coin operated laundromat, where *hot* and *cold* were the only options.

Amalia called from somewhere in the vast home. "I'm leaving now, Lillian."

Wait. I needed some instructions. As well as phone numbers. I knew that much from my teen babysitting years, when I didn't like kids, either.

"Amalia? When will you be back? And what else do I need to know?"

As I heard the front door open, I ran for it.

She thrust a couple twenties at me. "Here's some cash to get dinner. Robbie loves chicken nuggets. And we'll be home in a couple hours."

She sighed impatiently. "Don't worry. Cal will be here if you have any questions or need anything."

"He's not going with you?"

She laughed. "No. The overnight security team will drive us and bring us back home. See ya," she sang, and pulled the door closed.

Overnight security?

I slunk back to work folding the last of the towels I'd washed, when Robbie appeared in the laundry room.

"My mother doesn't like my coming in here," he said matter of factly. "I'm not allowed."

"Where? Here in the laundry room?"

He nodded.

"Why? It's just a laundry room."

"She says it's no place for a child."

Okay, that was fucking weird.

"Then let's get out of here, if you're not supposed to be in here. Geez, are you trying to get me in trouble?"

Robbie giggled.

"He will test you, as you've just experienced."

Security had appeared in the kitchen.

Whatever. At least he wouldn't try to cop a cheap feel.

"C'mon, Robbie. Show me where all these towels go," I said, heading for the stairs.

"No!" he yelled.

Well then.

"I want chicken nuggets!" he hollered.

I stopped and turned to him. "That's fine. We'll go get nuggets. *After* I put the laundry away."

That shut him right up. Did they have no boundaries with this kid?

"You're a natural," Security said, leaning in the kitchen doorway, smiling with his arms crossed.

Yeah, and you're a douche.

I was done five minutes later, when I found Robbie waiting by the door. I took his hand. "C'mon. Let's go."

"Excuse me."

Robbie and I both turned to see Security standing in the foyer, arms crossed.

"What?" I asked.

"You can't just walk out of the house," he said.

Wanna watch me?

I pulled the door open, when Robbie stopped me. "It's true. He comes with us."

Great. Just great.

"Well, c'mon then," I said.

"Were you just going to leave without a key or anything?" he asked, once we were in the elevator.

Really dude?

I shrugged. "I guess. I figured you'd be here when we got back."

Robbie pressed the button for the ground floor and jumped up and down singing *nuggets, nuggets*.

Security and I were silent until we passed the doorman, a stocky guy with gelled hair and an extreme New York accent.

"Hey, Stu. How are ya this evening?" Security said with a wave.

"Good, Cal, good. Hey, you going out for a walk?"

Robbie jumped and shouted. "Stu, we're getting nuggets."

Stu laughed, shaking his head, and turned back to what looked like his security cameras.

As soon as we hit the sidewalk, Security turned to me. "I'll walk with you but remain discreet."

Great.

What was I supposed to say? *Thank you, Mister Security?*

"C'mon Robbie. There's a McDonald's a few blocks away."

We set out, dodging the evening crowds, while Robbie babbled away about one thing or another.

I, however, was distracted by Security. First he'd walk ahead of us for a while, then behind us, and then next to us.

He was making me dizzy.

His eyes were scanning the whole time—the other pedestrians, traffic, bicyclists, taxis.

Seemed like overkill, if you asked me. Who the hell was this family that they needed all this guarding?

Dude was acting like a freaking Secret Service agent.

So I asked him while we waited in line at McDonald's. "What's this all about? This security stuff? Anything I need to know?" I asked with a small laugh.

"Robbie's dad, Eckhart von Malsen, is a very prominent diplomat."

Oh. Okay. Like New York wasn't full to the brim of important people.

Whatever.

Once back home, Robbie inhaled his nuggets and then I let him watch a PG-13 movie.

Because I could.

The von Malsens returned just when Amalia had promised. Thank god, because I was exhausted.

Housekeeping wasn't for the faint of heart. I wish I could have worked up to a full day of scrubbing, cleaning, and lugging shit around, like you did when you started a new exercise program. But it didn't seem to work that way.

"Eckie," Amalia sang, grabbing the arm of the man who I assumed was her husband, the esteemed diplomat, "please meet our new housekeeper, Lillian. This is the girl so highly recommended by Beebie."

Beebie the liar.

"Good to meet you, Lillian," he said, extending his hand.

He had much warmer eyes than his wife.

"Hello, Mr. von Malsen—"

He chuckled. "Please, Lillian, call me Eckie."

"Please call me Lill, then," I said.

Finally. Someone nice in the household.

"Thank you for filling in for the nanny on such short notice."

Yeah, yeah.

"My pleasure."

He looked at Security, who'd suddenly appeared out of nowhere. "Cal will take you home."

Like hell he will.

I grabbed my bag and slung it over my shoulder. "I'm fine with the subway. Thanks, though."

Eckie looked at his wife and smiled. "Okay, then. We'll let you both show yourselves out. Goodnight."

"See you Monday," Amalia sang, looking at Security with a lingering glance.

Jesus.

I headed for the door, and just as I was about to pull it shut behind me, Security slipped through it, joining me in the hallway.

Great.

I walked to the elevator ahead of him, pretending to be busy with my phone.

"At least let me walk you to the subway stop. I'll feel a lot better."

Should I tell him his feelings were none of my concern?

"Sure. That's fine."

I may have to work with the guy for a while. Best not to be a total bitch.

We walked to the subway in silence, and when I reached the top of the steps, I started down them.

"Goodnight, Lill. See you Monday."

"See ya," I said, waving over my shoulder.

He was probably planning how he'd cop another free feel.

CHAPTER 3

Callum 'Cal' Deverall

So pretty.

And such a bitch.

I could understand Lill's being put out that she had to be searched for weapons. And to be honest, if we were really following protocol, there would have been a female security operative to do the pat down.

But we didn't have a female to do the job, so it fell on me.

Not that I'm complaining.

But she was pretty fucking pissy about it. I mean, what did she think was going to happen in a top diplomat's home? They'd give her a key and free run of the place?

And to emphasize her displeasure, she'd stomped around the von Malsens' apartment, muttering under her breath the entire day.

Like a petulant brat.

Which kind of turned me on. I wouldn't mind the opportunity to straighten out her attitude. Like right over my knee. There was something about women who thought they were above the rules that got my motor revving.

And my dick hard.

I had to admit, though, I wouldn't want to clean someone's house. That'd put me in a bad mood, too.

What was she doing at the von Malsens', anyway? It wasn't every day you saw a tall, slender stunner like her running around a home on the Upper East Side, wearing yellow rubber gloves and carrying a bucket of cleaning supplies.

There was a story there. And I was going to find out what it was.

Still, she was one rude motherfucker. Hopefully, she'd taken the weekend to cool her jets and wouldn't be such a pain in the ass today.

Because, Monday.

Mondays were hard. Mondays sucked. Mondays meant I had to get back into the swing of things after a weekend off—no different from any other working stiff, really—but it also meant I needed to put together a brief of all the von Malsens' comings and goings and plan for their security needs for the week.

I'd thought I was done with paperwork when I'd left the force.

Wrong.

"Cal," the building's doorman called to me as I arrived at seven a.m. He glanced around to make sure no one else was in the lobby but us, and let the formality of his job slip away for a moment, giving me that half-hug half-handshake guys did with their friends. "Dude, did you see the Yankees this weekend? Fucking blew it out. Hey, Mr. Downing from the fifth floor gave me two tickets to tonight's game. Are ya free?"

"Damn. I wish I were. Sounds like a good time."

Stu shrugged, disappointed. "Well, if I can't find anyone else, I guess I could always take my girlfriend."

Jesus. Was taking your girlfriend that bad?

I shrugged. "You know I'm usually good for last minute, but I can't pull off tonight. Thanks, though."

"Hey, who's that hot new girl working for the von Malsens? You should have seen how annoyed she was when I had her sign in. Whew, what a handful you got there."

He wasn't kidding.

"Her name is Lillian—I mean, Lill. She's the new housekeeper."

Stu wrinkled his face like I knew he would. He saw plenty of staff coming and going in the building. People who lived in a place like this had lots of other folks do shit for them.

"Huh. I took her for a music teacher. Something artsy like that. Especially when she got all uppity about signing in. Have fun with that one, dude. She seems like a major PIA."

How right he was about that.

Stu put his finger up. "Hey, one more thing before you take off. The new folks living up in the penthouse are looking for a security guy. If you're looking to make a move, this could be a good opportunity."

"Thanks for the heads up. I'm sticking with von Malsen. He's a good guy. But I'll keep it in mind if I hear of anyone looking."

The people in the building were always trying to poach each others' staff.

"All right then, Cal. Have fun with your new redhead. God, I've always had a thing for them."

Yeah, she was going to be a load of fun.

I hated to miss the Yankees, but duty called. The von Malsens' security needs were in flux, and I was responsible for making sure any gaps were filled. We'd recently added weekend and night coverage because of alarming new intelligence from the security team over at the United Nations. Basically, Eckhart von Malsen's positions on global warming were not popular among some factions, and some of those folks were pretty extremist.

It was up to me to shore up their security coverage and to keep the family safe.

Which was why I was meeting my old friend Dex for beers after work.

⁂

I pulled open the massive wooden door of Regulator, one of the oldest bars in Manhattan, and peered into the dim light, my eyes slowly adjusting. Dex was behind the bar as usual, restocking beer for the night bartender.

"Hey, man," he called when he saw me. "Grab a booth. I'll be right over."

I liked Regulator. Something about it reminded me of the down-home bars in my old neighborhood in Cleveland. When I was a kid, every now and then, my mother would send me out to bring my dad home, who was usually hanging out with friends and having a couple. I loved those places because every time I went into one, his buddies would give me a dime or quarter.

I thought that if Dad kept hanging out at bars, I might be rich someday.

Dex set two IPAs on the table and slipped into the booth across from me.

I took a draw on my cold beer. "Damn, this is good. I was thinking about it all day."

Dex laughed. "You must have had a slow day."

I set my bottle down. "It wasn't slow at all, actually. And that's part of what I wanted to talk to you about."

He rubbed his hand over the beard covering his chin. "What do I have to do with your busy day?"

I had to laugh. He knew what was coming. We had the same conversation every six months or so.

"I need you to join my team, Dex."

He looked down at his beer and smiled, watching the ring of condensation under his bottle spread over the old, pockmarked table.

"Cal. I appreciate your thinking of me. But that's not my thing anymore." He gestured around the room. "I got this place to keep me busy. And I am *very* busy."

I took a deep breath. I knew recruiting him wasn't going to be easy. "Look, Dex, it wouldn't be a long-term thing, and it would be very lucrative. You have Jen to keep things running here. And I really need a man with your skills. My client is a high profile man, and he's going through a rough patch, politically."

He slowly shook his head.

But I was that hard to say no to.

"Man, why do you do this to me?" he asked with a laugh.

"Because I'm a pain in the ass?"

He pinched the bridge of his nose. "You really are. You know I left that shit behind. I made my money and cashed out. It's how I opened this joint. Regulator is my life now. I'm happy. I don't need anything else."

"Look, you made Jen part-owner so you'd have the flexibility to take off when you needed."

"I made Jen part-owner because she'd worked here

twenty years and knew more about running the place than I did."

We were both quiet for a moment.

Maybe it was wrong to pressure Dex the way I was. Pulling friends into my world hadn't always worked out too well. After all, my former partner in the force, whom I'd talked into joining, was no longer with us.

It still hurt every time I thought about it.

Fuck it. I'd put my feelers out for some new talent. I had no business dragging Dex out of the life he loved so much.

He picked at the corners of the label on his bottle. "How much does it pay?"

Was he actually considering it?

"Dex, it pays well. Really well. Like *fuck you money*, well."

"Jesus. Where do these people get their goddamn money?" he asked.

I shrugged. I didn't know. Didn't want to know.

"Don't do it just for the money, Dex. Think of it as a favor. I can't do this without you."

He chuckled and looked around the bar as if for an escape from my persistence. "All right," he said.

"All right?" I asked.

Had I heard him correctly?

He smiled. "Yes, I'll do it, for fuck's sake."

CHAPTER 4

Cal

My next stop was downtown. *Way* downtown.

I maneuvered my Jeep into a tight spot on the street and looked around before walking away. Car break-ins were rife in this neighborhood, but unless I sat in the damn vehicle, protecting it with my gun, there was little I could do to stop them. If the Jeep was broken into, so be it. It wouldn't be the first time, nor the last.

I dialed my cell.

"Hello?"

"Hey. I'm down here. Out front," I said.

"Be right there."

I watched a sketchy crowd of tweakers and hookers

flow in and out of the bowling alley Thorn lived above. I had a feeling there was a lot more business going on there besides renting shoes and bowling lanes. But that was not for me to worry about.

My friend Thorn was a different story, though.

A forbidding metal door scraped open, and Thorn stuck his head out. He looked up and down the street, more as a reflex than anything, and gestured for me to follow him inside.

"Cal, my man. How goes it?" he asked, his leather jacket shiny in the cheap fluorescent lights of the hallway.

"I'm good, man. You?"

He led the way past a broken elevator, into a stairwell, and we started to climb. Every time I'd ever been there, the elevator had been out of order.

"Shithole," he said, kicking an old container of Chinese food out of our way. "People live like goddamn pigs."

What a contrast Thorn's place was to the von Malsens'. The dichotomy that was New York devastated me sometimes.

Going from a multi-million dollar apartment on the Upper East Side, that was larger than many single family homes, to Thorn's place over a drug-infested bowling alley was, well, pretty indescribable.

I took a seat on the futon that also served as his bed, and he turned around a wooden dining chair to sit on it backwards and face me.

"It's good to see you, man."

The harsh overhead lamp swung lightly in the draft generated by the opening and closing of the door. Its glow reflected off the portion of Thorn's scalp that he'd shaved for an undercut, the shine stopping on the patch of hair he'd let grow on top of his head.

"You staying out of trouble?" I asked.

Thorn rolled his eyes. "Yeah, man. You know all that shit is behind me now."

"What are you doing for work?"

He frowned. "I didn't know you were my fucking probation officer."

Okay. Time for another approach.

"Thorn, I'm not here to check up on you. I'm here to talk to you about a job."

His eyebrows rose with interest. "I have a job. Coaching kids' basketball. But tell me about your offer."

He eyed me suspiciously. Couldn't blame him. He was about as street smart as they came, and you don't get that way by trusting people.

"Do you like it? Coaching?" I asked.

I needed to take his temperature first.

His expression softened. "I do. The kids are fucking awesome. Doesn't pay much though. In case you couldn't tell." He gestured to his apartment, which could easily fit inside the von Malsens' master bathroom.

"I have a way for you to make more money. A lot more money."

He raised his hands to the *stop* position. "No man. I'm done with that shit. I'm on the straight and narrow now."

"Thorn, that's not what I'm talking about," I said with a chuckle.

"Then what are you talking about?"

"I handle private security for a prominent family here. I need help."

He sat up straight in his chair. "Help? What kind of help?"

"Well, I need someone like you. Someone with street smarts, who's a big motherfucker, and who can shoot if necessary."

He thought for a moment. "Okay. Keep going."

"And it pays a fuckload. You could be out of this place right away. If you wanted."

I shouldn't have assumed he'd want to move. Maybe he felt comfortable in his modest but familiar surroundings.

"What's the catch?" he asked.

Good question.

"There isn't one, as least that I can think of."

Unless you wanted to consider Lill a drawback.

Or was she a benefit?

Thorn looked down at his hands. "Dude, my brother's always trying to get me to come back. I tell him no, but it's not easy."

"I know, Thorn. I know."

The temptation to get back into street crime, and make relatively easy money, was a big draw. I mean, shit, if it wasn't appealing we wouldn't have so many criminals. Maybe with an offer that would earn him enough to improve his standard of living, any temptation would fall by the wayside.

"I need your help, Thorn. And if it makes any difference, there's a really beautiful girl who also works for the family. She's a smart-mouthed ball buster. Just how we like 'em."

He laughed.

"Okay, you asshole. I'm in."

CHAPTER 5

Lill

I was learning that the good thing about cleaning every day was that a place didn't have a chance to really ever get dirty to begin with. So, there was that.

Why hadn't I realized that about my own apartment? Instead of going for weeks and sometimes months without cleaning, and then scrubbing my fingers raw when I finally did, I could have just kept up with it.

Yeah, like I would ever do that.

I pulled the vacuum out of the closet and ran it over the guest bedroom carpet, which still had the vacuum marks in it from the day before. But like Amalia said, keep ahead of it, and it wouldn't be hard work.

How did she know anything about cleaning?

So, with my earbuds in, I pushed the vacuum back and forth making new marks on the plushy carpet, when someone tapped me on the shoulder.

I screeched.

I pulled an earbud out. "Oh my gosh, Amalia. Sorry. You startled me."

Apparently my scream had startled her, too. She brought her hand to her chest while she caught her breath.

"Didn't mean to scare you so badly, Lill. It's just that you couldn't hear me calling you over the vacuum and your music."

"It was actually a podcast. *This American Life.*"

Yeah, I listened to public radio.

Which clearly surprised Amalia. Apparently, she didn't think cleaning people who were aspiring writers listened to NPR.

"Super," she said with disinterest. "Can you run to the cleaners please? Here's the receipt and some cash to pay for Eckie's shirts and a couple things of mine." She pressed everything into my hand before I could say anything.

"Sure," I said, and started wrapping up the vacuum cord while Amalia disappeared.

I grabbed my jacket and headed for the door after putting the vacuum away.

"Where are you going?" Robbie demanded, stepping in front of me in the foyer.

I had half a mind to tell him to fuck off. He wasn't my problem today.

"I'm going to the cleaners for your mother." I reached for the door.

"I WANT TO COME," he screeched.

Oh, god.

"I WANT A BALLOON," he screeched.

At this rate, I wouldn't buy him a balloon if he were the last child on earth.

"No, Robbie. I'll be right back. We don't have time to shop for balloons."

"MOMMY!"

Fuck.

Amalia poked her head out from the top of the stairs. "Robbie, why are you shouting?"

He lowered his voice, putting on a sweet smile. "Momma, can Lill take me for a balloon?"

"Oh, sure. Go ahead, Lill." And she disappeared again.

Ugh.

"All right. Let's go. But you have to hold my hand. If you don't, we're coming right back home."

"Yay," he said, jumping up and down.

"Hold it there."

I turned to find Security scowling at Robbie and me. Shit, what had I done wrong now? Did he think I was stealing the little brat? Because he could have him.

"Robbie, I think Cal wants you to stay here." I reached for the door again.

"NO!" he screamed.

Security pressed his lips together and walked over to me. "You can take him. It's just that I need to go."

Ohforchristssake.

"Really?"

What was this, a fucking party? A field trip? An entourage? I just wanted to pick up the von Malsens' dry cleaning and get back to listening to *This American Life*. And cleaning.

Frustration washed over his face and for a moment I felt like a dipshit. But only for a moment.

"You know I have to come," he said, looking down at me. Very closely.

A gorgeous hunk of a security man following me around the Upper East Side. If it wasn't so bizarre, it would be hot.

"Okay, c'mon everyone. Let's get going." I led Robbie out the door by the hand. Security could keep up on his own.

I was tempted to put my ear buds back in so I wouldn't have to listen to either one of them, but that seemed unwise. What if Robbie told his mother? No doubt he was the tattling type.

So first we swung by a stationery store that had balloons. Robbie agonized over his color choice for so long that I caved and bought him two.

It wasn't like I was paying for them.

Then we headed to the cleaners. And it turned out

having Security along, despite all his crowd scanning, was not so bad. He was also good for carrying stuff.

I never could have done it on my own.

As we made our way back, Robbie babbled happily, talking to his new balloons. Security was somewhere behind us—I wasn't paying attention—and I was thinking ahead to the evening's writing class where I'd head right after work.

It wasn't easy being a romance author in a writing class. Most of the people were pretty snooty and looked down on anything written mainly for women.

Fuck 'em was my feeling. I was learning a lot about becoming a solid storyteller, and the instructor often praised my work.

Which pissed off the literary snobs in the class.

In tonight's class, my sort-of friend Bert would be reading pages from his latest work in progress—something about the resistance in World War II France. I wasn't much interested but I'd play along like I was. It was what we were expected to do.

As I broke a sweat, I was happy to see the von Malsens' building in view. I had several plastic dry cleaning bags draped over one arm, even though Cal had taken the bulk of them. With my other hand, I was trying to hold on to Robbie while he was making a big show of jumping over every crack in the sidewalk.

I turned at the sound of a car coming to a screeching stop at the curb next us, in order to drop off a passenger. Damn, those New York taxis drove like maniacs.

But it wasn't a taxi.

And the man getting out wasn't a passenger.

As if in slow motion, he locked eyes with me and ran toward us. For a moment I assumed I knew him, and he was coming to say hello. Just as I was wracking my brains to figure out who he might be, he grabbed Robbie by the arm and started pulling him away.

Why would he want Robbie?

The kid went into full-on screeching mode, not because he was being pulled from me by some stranger, but because the balloons had slipped out of his grip and floated out of reach before I could think to retrieve them.

Robbie was pulled out of my grip before I could think to retrieve him, too.

What the fucking fuck?

I dropped all the dry cleaning on the sidewalk and lunged after Robbie, just missing his free hand. But I saw the dark eyes of the guy pulling him away, as well as the shaded face of the car's driver.

And like that, it was over.

Mister Security had moved fast enough to scoop Robbie out of the arms of the strange man, who, when he realized he'd been bested, jumped back into the car, which peeled away from the curb leaving skid marks on the street.

I couldn't speak. My arms hung at my sides, shaking

uncontrollably, while the von Malsens' dry cleaning started to blow around the sidewalk.

Security ran up to me with the screaming Robbie in his arms. "C'mon," he said, grabbing my hand and running toward the building.

"But the cleaning—" I protested, still not making sense of what was happening.

"Forget the clothes," he shouted, yanking me back to my senses.

Once inside, he handed Robbie to me and peered back out the doors.

"Stu, can you do me a favor?" he asked the doorman. "Someone just tried to abduct Robbie. The von Malsens' dry cleaning is all over the sidewalk. Can you pick it up for me and bring it upstairs?"

Stu hopped to his feet and headed for the door. "Sure, Cal. I got it."

I looked at him as he began dialing his phone. "Um, Cal? Did you say abducted? Like someone tried to abduct Robbie?"

It had all happened so fast I couldn't process it.

"Yes, Lill. Someone tried to abduct Robbie."

He started speaking to someone on the phone in a low voice.

Unsure what to do, I made my way to the elevator. Robbie was still pissed about losing his balloons and was trying to squirm out of my arms. Just as the elevator doors began to close and take us upstairs, a big hand reached between them and pulled them back open.

"Stick with me," Security said, pressing the button for the von Malsens' floor.

"Thank you."

"Hmmm?" he said, turning toward me.

I cleared my throat and tried not to mumble. "Thank you. Thank you for saving Robbie."

He just looked ahead and nodded. And I felt like an asshole.

CHAPTER 6

Lill

"Where's Robbie?" a male voice called.
Footsteps clicked through the foyer and into the living room.

"Robbie!" Eckie shouted.

"We're in the kitchen, Mr. von Malsen," I called, waving from the door.

He sprinted across the floor and scooped Robbie into his arms, burying his face in his hair.

It was so intimate I thought I should look away. So I busied myself cleaning up the milk and cookies I'd just let Robbie snack on. I knew dinner would be soon, but I didn't know what the hell else to do with the kid until the night nanny arrived.

"Mr. von Malsen—"

"Please Lill, call me Eckie. And I don't know how I will ever thank you and Cal for saving Robbie. I don't know what Amalia and I would have done if—"

His voice broke and he buried his face in Robbie's hair.

Holy shit. What had I gotten myself into?

"Well, um, Eckie. Cal is the one who deserves the thanks."

I looked at Cal, who pressed his lips together and nodded his appreciation.

"It was close, Eckie. I'm having the new guys on the security team start tomorrow. For the time being, none of you can go out without one of us. Okay?"

Something about Cal's barking instructions struck me as hot. So authoritative and confident. Like he could handle anything that came his way.

I was going to try not to mock him anymore. *Try*.

I didn't know many guys like Cal, especially not among the 'sensitive' ones in my writing group.

Eckie looked around frantically. "Where's Amalia? Has anybody seen her?"

Oh. Shit.

"I… I haven't seen her. Have you, Cal? She sent me to the cleaners so she could run some other errands. I don't know where she went."

Cal frowned. "Are you sure she went out? She didn't say anything to me."

I shook my head slowly. "I'm pretty sure she did. But I don't know where."

Cal started dialing his phone again, while Eckie looked on, terrified.

"No answer," he said after a minute. He set his phone on the marble countertop and crossed his arms, frowning.

I went upstairs to avoid further family drama, and got back to my vacuuming. I wanted to leave the place in good shape before I quit.

I had no idea what sort of curse was hanging over this household, but I didn't need this shitshow in my life. I went down to the laundry room to grab the last of the towels, and just as I was thinking of a graceful way to bail, the front door blew open.

"I'm home," Amalia called.

Still holding Robbie in a death grip, Eckie called, "In here, honey."

"Oh. Hello, everyone," Amalia said from the kitchen doorway. "Eckie, what are you doing home?"

He and Cal spilled the story of everything that had happened. I only half listened, preoccupied as I was with how I was going to quit without making Beebie, who'd recommended me to the von Malsens, look bad.

Then they turned to me.

"Lill, can you tell the exact story of what happened, in your own words?" Cal asked. "And if you could stick around a bit longer, I'm having someone come by to do a forensic sketch of the guy you saw."

"Didn't you just explain everything that happened already?" I asked.

But from the look on his face, he wasn't messing around. So I essentially repeated what Cal had said, just from my point of view.

"Goodness," Amalia said breezily. "Well, it looks like everything worked out just fine."

She smiled and kissed Robbie on the forehead.

Okay, that was fucking weird. She was not in the least worked up about her kid almost being taken.

Shit just keeps getting deeper.

"What do you want for dinner tonight, honey? Nuggets again?" Amalia asked, pulling Robbie out of Eckie's arms.

She'd better not ask me to take him to McDonald's.

"I can't thank you enough," Eckie said to Cal, extending his hand for a shake. "Can you accompany Lill home tonight? If she saw the kidnappers, she might not be safe."

What? Me? Not safe?

"Oh, that's okay, Eckie, I'm fine on the subway."

"No, Lill, you are not," Cal said sternly.

Damn if that didn't send a shiver down my spine.

"Well. Okay," I said. "Let me finish upstairs."

In the car, Cal didn't utter a word after he asked me for the address of my apartment. The night's writing class was long over and I'd missed it, trying to remember the face of a man I saw for maybe a couple seconds.

"Thanks for driving me, Cal. It's probably not necessary, but I appreciate it. You're saving me subway fare," I joked.

He pulled up in front of my building. "Lill. You saw the two men who tried to grab Robbie. Do you have any idea what that means?"

"Well, you saw them too, right?"

He sighed. "I didn't see either of their faces. By the time I'd grabbed Robbie, the guy had made a run for the car."

"Oh. Geez."

"Besides, I can defend myself. I've got a gun. You do not."

Right.

"Yeah," I said in a small voice. "Well, I'll go in now. Thanks again."

"Hold on," he said, turning the car off. "I'm going up with you. I want to check your place."

I wrinkled my nose. "Oh, I don't think that's necessary, Cal—"

But before I could finish, he was around my side of the car, and gestured for me to go first.

Okay. If it would make him feel better to look over my apartment before he left, well, then he was welcome to. It was no skin off my back.

"How long have you lived here?" he asked as we climbed the stairs to the second floor.

"About a year and a half," I said. "It's a good location.

And my rent is pretty decent. For New York, anyway," I babbled.

I pulled out my key and began to insert it into the deadbolt when Cal stopped me.

"Here. Let me do it. I want to go first."

"Okay. The light is on the wall to the left."

He pushed my door open, flicked the light, and peered inside.

"Shit," he growled.

"What?" I asked, pushing him aside and looking around. "No!"

My apartment had been ransacked.

Trashed.

Completely.

CHAPTER 7

Dexter 'Dex' Brooks

"Lill needs help."

Jesus. Cal hadn't been kidding when he said things were heating up for his clients.

"Okay. Where is she?" I asked.

His voice was tight. I knew that tone. It wasn't good. "She's heading downtown on the 6 Line. Sounds like there's some suspicious guy on the train."

Shit. What the hell was she doing on the subway?

"She has three more stops until she exits. Can you meet her train?" Cal asked.

I turned the car around. Luckily for all of us, I was already in the vicinity of downtown. "Yup. I'm on it."

Then I remembered I'd never met her. "Dude, I don't even know—"

"You'll know her. She has this wild, long red hair. I've never seen anything like it. Tall and curvy. She'll probably look scared shitless. I'll tell her to look for you outside the turnstile."

"I'm on it."

"Thanks. I'll text you when she's there."

After running through a few yellow traffic lights, and one red, I pulled my car over to the first spot I saw open. I ran to Lill's subway stop and sprinted down the stairs, where I waited.

I'd gotten there just in time for the arrival of a train, judging by the sound of the doors whooshing open and closed, and the flood of exiting people coming toward me.

she's coming, Cal texted me.

I stretched to see over the crowd, and saw a redhead running right toward me.

Holy shit. Cal didn't tell me she looked like *this*.

And from the expression on her face, it appeared that the full weight of the predicament she was in, and what a close call she'd just had, finally had made an indelible impression on her. She ran, terrified, nearly right into my arms.

"Oh my god. You're Dex, right?" she asked breathlessly, peering up at me.

I looked around. "Do you see any other big black guys waiting at the subway for you?" I took her hand as if we were being introduced, but held on to it, hoping it would calm her shaking.

Her face softened a little and tears sprang to her eyes. "Dumb question. I'm not thinking straight at the moment."

"I don't blame you, sweetie. But you're safe now. C'mon, let me take you home."

She was scared shitless. As she should be.

"Here, take my arm," I said, extending my elbow.

"Thank you. My friend's apartment, where I'm staying, is just a few blocks away."

I wouldn't normally expect a client to hold on to me minutes after we'd just met, but it was clear she desperately needed comforting. She didn't know me from a hole in the wall, aside from the fact that Cal had sent me, and yet she had to trust me. Shit like that wasn't easy when you're terrified.

"Lill, why don't you tell me what happened in the subway. And why you were on it, anyway."

She looked at me and nodded, scanning the sidewalk and street. When I knew her better, I'd tell her that was my job. Until then, she needed to do whatever she could to feel better. To gain a bit of control over a crazy situation.

It was natural. Those of us in private security saw this type of reaction all the time.

First, people are in denial.

I'm fine. I don't need anybody...

Then, reality sets in.

Holy shit. Help...

"Okay. I was coming home from my writing class, riding the train with my friend Bert."

Hmmm. Had we checked out *Bert*?

"Who's this Bert guy?"

She waved her hand. "Oh, just this annoying guy in my class. He's always trying to date me."

It wasn't hard to see why. In fact, when I first saw Lill running out of the subway, I'd kind of hoped she was the person I was supposed to be waiting for.

Unprofessional, yes. But c'mon. She was fucking beautiful with all that red hair flying behind her.

"So we're on the train. He was babbling away about himself like he always does, and there was a guy at the end of the car who kept staring. Something about it felt weird. Really off."

"Did he look familiar?" I asked.

She shook her head. "No. Definitely not. But he kept looking at me and the other people on the train like he was sizing everyone up."

"What did your friend Bert do? While this was going on?"

"He was oblivious. Like always. Anyway, when the train stopped, Bert stayed on because he lives in Brooklyn, and I ran full speed toward you, just as Cal instructed."

I stopped and looked around the street. There was no one in sight. If someone had been following Lill, he probably hadn't been assigned to carry anything out, thank god. He was likely just watching her.

We stopped in front of an expensive-looking high rise. I could easily identify the nicer buildings around because I lived in one, myself.

"Did he follow you off the train?" I asked.

She pressed her lips together and looked behind us again. "I don't think so. I ran out the subway door just as it was closing to try and get rid of him."

I bit my tongue to keep from laughing. She'd been watching way too much TV. But I had to hand it to her. She was gutsy in the face of something pretty fucking scary.

"This is my friend Beebie's building, where I'm staying since my own place was broken into. Thank you so much, Dex. I was freaking. I don't know what's going on or how I got roped into this. It's all strange. I just want to do my job and be left alone to write."

Right, Cal had told me she was a writer.

"I'm sorry, Lill. You were just in the wrong place at the wrong time when the von Malsen kid was almost abducted."

She rolled her eyes as her mojo slowly returned. "Just my damn luck. I swear to god. I hadn't even been working for those people one week when all this rained down on my head."

As her fear dissipated, the feistiness Cal warned me about began showing itself.

And I loved it. A ballsy chick? That's what I wanted all day, every day.

"I'll be back tomorrow morning to pick you up," I said, looking around the building lobby to assess its security. Cameras, coded elevators, and a doorman passed the test. Much better than the building she'd been living in, which Cal said had only a rickety entrance door and dim hallways. "What were you doing on the subway, anyway? Hadn't Cal explained that you were to get picked up and dropped off?"

She looked guilty. "Yeah. But I thought since I was taking the subway with a guy friend, it would be okay. Guess not, huh?"

I just looked at her while it all sank in.

She squeezed my hand. "Thank you, Dex. I appreciate it. I'm sorry for all this trouble."

"Don't apologize, Lill. Mr. von Malsen is paying us to protect you. Just like he is the rest of his family. He knows you wouldn't be in this position if it weren't for him."

Resignation crossed her face. "So he thinks I'm in danger too, huh?"

"He knows you are."

CHAPTER 8

Dex

Cal hadn't been kidding when he'd called his friend Thorn rough around the edges. I was reminded of that every time I saw him. He was one of the guys who, in the private security world, were called 'fixers,' and that night he strolled into Regulator wearing dark aviators and a well-broken-in leather jacket, a single braid sticking out of the top of his otherwise shaved head.

"Good to see you, Dex," he said, extending his hand for a shake. He looked around the bar. "This your place?"

"Yeah. Well, mine and my co-owner, Jen's. I'm kind

of on a leave of absence, though, since I'm helping Cal with this latest job."

"Hey guys. What can I bring you?" Jen asked.

"This is Thorn," I said, gesturing across the table.

His face brightened. "Very nice to meet you, ma'am," he said, looking her up and down.

Uh oh.

She scowled at him like I knew she would.

"I'll have a Stella," I said.

"And I'll have a Maker's Mark," Thorn said. "Three fingers."

Jen rolled her eyes and left.

"Wow, she's your co-owner. How do you keep your hands off her?" Thorn said, following her every move.

"Well, first of all, she doesn't play for our team. And second, I respect her."

Thorn's eyes widened. He realized he'd overstepped his bounds. I had to give him credit for that. A lot of meathead guys had no self-awareness whatsoever.

He rested his arms on the table. "Sorry, man. I've been holed up, staying out of sight for so long that I've forgotten how to behave."

"You were one of Cal's informers when he was on the force, right? I don't think I've seen you in more than a year. What are you up to now?" I asked.

"When Cal left the force, I decided to go clean. He helped me. I couldn't have done it without him. I'm coaching kids' basketball now."

Shit. I'd known Cal was a good guy, but getting

someone off the streets was next to impossible. He'd practically worked a miracle.

"That's great, Thorn. Congrats," I said, taking a draw on the beer Jen had dropped off.

"And you know him from college, right?" he asked.

"Yeah, we were in college together. After an injury, I lost my football scholarship, so I left school and joined the military. We always kept in touch, though."

School. The bane of my existence. That unfinished degree had hung over my head for longer than I cared to admit.

I looked down at my beer. "I never finished. I kept thinking I would, but a private security team recruited me out of the military. It paid so well I couldn't say no."

I'd always thought I'd go back and finish my coursework, but life kept getting in the way.

He nodded. "Nice, man. That's why I'm here. Cal said I could make some serious dough. More than I make coaching kids' basketball, that's for sure. And maybe get out of my roach-infested dump of an apartment."

"Guys. Sorry I'm late," Cal said, breathing hard. He dropped his crossbody bag onto the seat and slid into the booth next to Thorn. "You guys remember each other, right?"

"We're old friends now," Thorn said, smiling. He stood. "Hey, gotta take a piss. Restrooms back there?" he asked pointing.

I nodded and watched him get up from the table. Jesus. The guy was huge.

Cal smiled as he watched Thorn walk away. "He's one of a kind, isn't he?"

"Yeah. But he seems like a good guy."

"He is. I wouldn't have stuck my neck out for him if I hadn't believed in him. He's come a long way." He shook his head for a second. "God, that sounds so patronizing. Like I saved his ass or something. Thorn saved himself."

I waved Jen over so Cal could order.

"So what'd you make of Lill?" he asked me.

"Well, she's a handful. Maybe I should leave it at that."

He laughed. "Agreed. Not sure whether I should tell her to go fuck herself, or ask her out to dinner."

That about summed it up.

He continued. "She can be a pain in the ass. I've been tempted to just let whoever's after her, catch her. But von Malsen wouldn't be very happy about that. Which is why we are all meeting here today."

"So, fill us in, boss," Thorn said, returning to the table.

Wait till Thorn got a load of Lill. His head would explode. Or something would.

Cal looked at us, all business. "As you know, someone tried to snatch my client's kid off the street the other day."

"Any idea who it was?" Thorn asked.

He ran his fingers through his short, preppy hair. "Yes and no. Von Malsen has made some enemies lately in the international community. However, I'm not sure how they knew where the kid would be the day we were out, nor where Lill lived so they could ransack her apartment, or even why, for that matter? Were they waiting for her to come home? Or just trying to scare the shit out of her? *That* seems like more of an inside job to me."

"What do you mean inside job?" I asked.

He shrugged. "I'm wondering if there is a disgruntled household employee, like a nanny or cook? I just don't know."

Thorn stood again. "I'm getting water. Anybody?" he asked, looking at Cal and me.

"I'll take another beer."

We sat in silence while I watched the women in the bar do double-takes over Thorn. He was mostly oblivious, which was pretty funny for a guy like him.

"Check it out," I said leaning toward Cal. "Women are fucking falling all over Thorn. They love a bad boy, don't they?"

Cal shook his head and laughed.

"Whoa. There are some serious beauties in this part of town," Thorn said when he returned, setting down our fresh drinks. "I need to come up here more often."

Cal had told me about the shithole bowling alley Thorn lived above. It sounded rough. I hoped this gig would help him toward a better situation.

"I'm telling you, Thorn," Cal said, "the further you get from the meth heads in your neighborhood, the better off you'll be."

"Isn't that the truth?" Thorn said, raising his glass in a toast. "I don't know how much longer I can jerk off to porn, man."

"You're on your way, my friend," Cal said, laughing. "Cheers."

"Speaking of being on our way, how'd you end up working for a bunch of rich fuckers? Who'd you blow to get that gig?" Thorn asked.

The man didn't beat around the bush, that was for damn sure.

Cal laughed. "I'd met von Malsen when I was on the force. He took a liking to me and convinced me to retire and come work for him. I thought it would be a cushy gig, something I needed after—well, you know—"

Cal cleared his throat the way guys do when they're holding back.

He'd never forgive himself for what happened to his partner.

"Anyway. Little did I know that diplomats can be pretty controversial people. I guess the shit that's following von Malsen is not that unusual."

I looked around the bar as I was in the habit of doing, which was approaching its usual post-happy hour clear out. "So when is our friend Lill arriving?" I asked.

"What is she like?" Thorn asked.

"Well, she's fucking beautiful, as Cal said. Tall with great curves with that crazy, wavy red hair and freckles. When I picked her up at the subway, she was shaken. But by the time we got to her friend's apartment, she was a regular ball-buster."

Cal nodded, smiling.

Thorn looked at him. "Somebody's got the hots for Lill," he joked.

I sure as hell wasn't the only one.

"Wait till you see her, is all I can say. Just wait," I said.

"Yeah, yeah. No one's that special," Thorn laughed.

I watched Cal's eyebrows rise. "Guys, it doesn't matter if you're head over heels with her. She's a client. Not a prospective wife."

Taking advantage of the view of the bar's front door from my seat, I watch it open and close in anticipation of her arrival. "She might not be a prospective wife, but I sure as hell wouldn't mind asking her to be."

CHAPTER 9

Lill

"Hey. What were you saying about a wife, Dex? Are you getting married?"

I plopped down on the seat next to him, scooting aside somebody's crossbody bag. I was fucking exhausted. Amalia had me cleaning light fixtures all day. Talk about a shit job. My arms were already killing me, and I knew they would be worse by morning.

He nearly choked on his beer. "Nope, not getting married."

"Huh. Could have sworn I'd heard you say something about a wife. Anyway, hi. I'm Lill," I said, extending my hand to the guy opposite.

Must have been Thorn, the friend Cal had told me

about. And damn if he wasn't one badass-looking dude. A complete contrast to Cal, who was as preppy as a Ralph Lauren ad, and Dex, who looked like an NFL running back.

The three of them together? Perfection.

Thorn extended his hand, which jingled with heavy silver rings. "Nice to meet you," he said quietly.

Dex and Cal looked his way.

What? Was there some joke I missed?

"Is something going on?" I asked, waving over a server for a glass of wine.

Jesus. In what world were security guys this beautiful? Seriously.

Here I was with the three guys who were here to protect my sorry little nobody ass. Just a cleaning lady for some rich Upper East Side family—and a sometime-substitute nanny—who wanted nothing more than to write stories and work for a cool magazine. I lived in a crappy studio apartment that was even crappier now that some fucker had broken into it and rifled through everything.

In the game of life, I was not hitting any home runs. Hell, I wasn't even getting on base.

I did have one really nice, expensive dress, though.

I gave myself credit for that. Now I wondered, when would I be able to wear it? I couldn't very well be a girl about town with a security detail trailing me.

Could I?

"How far do we need to go with this security stuff?

Like will you be following me everywhere for the rest of my life? That could be kind of awkward." I tried to laugh but it came out sounding choked.

I didn't mean to sound ungrateful. I definitely liked the idea of having someone to call when some creep in the subway was freaking me out, or someone was trying to kidnap the kid I was minding. But every day?

Seemed a little like overkill. But on the other hand, I liked the idea of staying alive. A Lot.

Cal took a deep breath. I was clearly frustrating him. But I had questions, dammit.

"Look, Lill. Even if we thought you were fine and that no one would ever bother you again, we couldn't cut you loose. Mr. von Malsen has hired us to keep you safe."

I shook my head. "I don't know why he would give a shit about my well-being. I mean, I just clean their bathrooms and pick up their dry-cleaning."

Cal looked at the other guys. Fine. They knew something I didn't.

"Eckie is a good man. He doesn't want anything to happen to you. That's partially out of the goodness of his heart, but it's also self-serving," Cal said.

God, the wine Jen had just brought me was good. For the first time all day, the knots in my neck were starting to melt away. Of course, sitting directly across from Cal and Thorn, and next to Dex, felt pretty fucking good too.

"What do you mean self-serving, Cal?"

He pressed his lips together. He was clearly about to share information he'd rather not.

"Think how it would look for one of Eckhart von Malsen's household staff to be hurt or killed, just because she was working for him."

Um.

Killed?

Well, that lent a new perspective.

Optics. Good old Eckie didn't want to look bad.

So he threw money at the problem.

Well, that, and three gorgeous men. I was cool with it.

This shit was definitely going to end up in one of my romance novels.

I pointed at all three guys. "I have to let you know that I have a job interview coming up. You cannot attend that with me."

I took another sip of my wine to signal *end of discussion*.

It didn't work.

"One of us will accompany you. No one will even know we are there."

Damn.

I sniffed. "Okay. Well, what if I have a date or something? Is one of you going to come along like a chaperone? Make sure I don't go *all the way?*"

I dropped my head back and laughed. A chaperone. Imagine that.

But the guys didn't laugh.

Shit.

So any date I was lucky enough to land in the foreseeable future would indeed include a third wheel. Great.

"Look, Lill," Dex started, "your friend Beebie's place is pretty secure. Stay there for the time being, until we figure out what we're up against. We'll pick you up and drop you off every day, and everyone will feel better knowing you're safe."

Cal nodded. "This is not a forever thing. We're working hard to identify the person or people who tried to kidnap Robbie and who wrecked your apartment."

"Don't forget the weirdo on the subway," I added.

"Yup. Him too," Cal said.

Well, shit. There was no way out of this bizarre situation in the immediate term. I'd just have to suck it up. Of course, I could always leave town and tell no one where I was going, but why should I be chased out just because a big diplomat is on some criminal's shit list?

What did I do wrong?

As if he could read my mind, Thorn piped in. "This is not your fault, you know. It's a pain in the ass, but there's not much you could have done to avoid the situation."

Dex nodded, turning in the booth to fully face me. I tried not to stare, but there was a huge bulge behind the fly of his blue jeans.

Jesus, Lill. Get a grip.

I supposed my situation could be a lot worse, starting with the kidnappers having gotten away with taking Robbie. If that had happened, it would be on me. I didn't need that sort of nuclear-level problem.

"Another option, Lill, is that you could stay at the von Malsens. Eckie offered a room with its own bathroom."

Over my dead fucking body.

"Cal, do you think I would *ever* agree to that? I know you've seen how Amalia treats me. There is just no way in hell that would work."

He shook his head in agreement. "I told Eckie I didn't think you'd be interested. I just wanted you to know the offer had been made."

I could appreciate a well-intended offer. But the answer was still no.

And besides, my world was now turned upside down because of that family. If Amalia hadn't asked me to go out for her dry cleaning and insist I take her rugrat for a balloon, none of this would be happening.

So, it was really all her fault.

And she probably couldn't give a shit.

CHAPTER 10

Lill

I woke up early the next morning, so sore I could barely pull a T-shirt over my head. I hoped by the next time I had to clean overhead lamps, I would have built up more muscle and stamina to avoid a repeat of this painful experience. I downed a small handful of Advil with Beebie's excellent imported coffee, and since I had about an hour before work, I started sending resumes to headhunters. It seemed they owned exclusive access to jobs at the city's best women's magazines.

Unless you knew someone, which I did not, or were otherwise well-connected, which I was not. If you were like me, you had to take the long route to getting a job.

Not that I was going to let that hold me back forever. I was getting out and *making connections*. That was part of the reason I'd spent the last of my cash on my bitching new dress.

The front door intercom buzzed, and I threw my laptop into my bag, just as Beebie stumbled out of her bedroom in her plushy cow-print bathrobe.

"Why're you up so early?" she yawned.

I looked over my shoulder as I headed to the door. "I wanted to send some resumes before I had to head uptown."

She poured herself coffee. "Any word on your apartment break in?"

Dex had told me to share as little as possible with Beebie in order to protect her—and the von Malsens, of course.

"Nope. Don't know a thing. Getting tired of me here?" I asked with laugh.

"Lill, you know better than that. I think you should just move in here permanently," she said.

Cripes. That would be the day. Beebie had one of the most beautiful places I'd ever seen. But I couldn't jeopardize our friendship that way. She meant way too much to me.

"All right, crazy girl. I'll keep that in mind."

"See ya," she said, waving over her shoulder as she pulled up the news on her iPad.

"Morning, Dex," I said, jumping into the von Malsens' SUV. Or *one* of their SUVs, anyway.

"Hey, Lill. Ready for another great day?" he asked, his brown skin more flawless than ever in the morning light.

He seemed like a nice guy, but I did hate him for that complexion. My own was marred with freckles that gave away my Irish roots. All the makeup in the world wouldn't hide those little buggers.

As for the day ahead, I wouldn't say I expected it to be anything in the great category. In fact, if it wasn't plain shitty, I'd be grateful for that.

"Sure am, Dex. Ready for another great day." I nearly choked on the words.

As we drove across town, I could barely take my eyes off his massive hands. It was like he had two baseball mitts at the ends of his arms and for a moment I imagined them smoothing over the curves of my ass...

Get a grip, girl.

He swerved to avoid a manic taxi and I put my hand on the dashboard to brace myself.

"Asshole," he mumbled under his breath.

"So you're a writer?" he asked.

I was about to say *aspiring writer. Wanna be writer. Working on becoming a writer*. But I didn't need those damn qualifiers.

I was a *writer*, dammit, plain and simple.

"Yeah. I am."

He steered into the von Malsens' parking garage. "That's cool. Really cool," he said, glancing at me with a killer smile.

Shit. I was in trouble.

"What do you write?" he asked when we were on our way up in the elevator.

"Romance. Romance novels."

He broke out in a grin. "No way. My mom was a fiend for romance stories. Want to know a little secret?" he asked, leaning closer.

"Okay."

God, he smelled good.

He lowered his voice even though no one was around. "When I was a kid, I read a couple of my mom's romances. Wanted to see what all the fuss was about."

The elevator doors opened, and we walked slowly toward the von Malsen's.

"What did you think?"

He bit his bottom lip. Was he embarrassed? "They're not the kind of thing that appeals to a twelve year old boy. But I was glad I gave them a whirl."

How. Freaking. Cute.

We stopped for a moment before entering. "I'll tell ya what. When one of my books is published, I promise to give you a copy. I'll even sign it."

He dropped his head back and laughed. "I'll hold you to that. Don't forget."

We entered the house laughing, and when I got to the kitchen, Amalia gave me a dirty look.

Because of course.

"Morning," I said tying an apron over my clothes.

Since I'd started work for the von Malsens, I'd developed a schedule for the cleaning: bathrooms on Mondays, floors on Tuesdays, beds on Wednesdays, etc. The rhythm was comfortable, even if being in Amalia's presence was not.

Oh, Lill. Hi. Hey, I wanted to tell you something."

"What's that?" I asked brightly.

"About the security measures Eckie insists you need. They're kind of ridiculous. I mean, who's going to go after *you*?"

Did she really just say that?

And when I saw the totally serious expression on her face, I realized that not only had she said that, but she fucking meant it, too.

I smiled at her. "Thanks Amalia. That's nice of you to say."

Her head twitched. "Oh. Well. I didn't mean any offense. Don't be so sensitive."

I reached under the sink to gather my cleaning supplies, wanting to get as far away from her as possible.

"Lill, I had an idea," she said, like she was throwing me a bone.

I pulled on my yellow rubber gloves. Why couldn't she just let me do my work without a conversation?

"I know a literary agent. He might be interested in talking to you about your romance novel."

What?

Did she actually just say something *nice* to me? That could potentially *help* me?

"You do?"

She nodded. She had me now.

Dammit.

"I'd be happy to make an introduction."

Holy shit. Was she for real?

"But you know what," she continued, "I'd really like to read your book, too. Now that charity season is over, I have more time. Plus, I haven't read a romance book in ages."

She read romance books? I hadn't seen a single one on any of the apartment's bookshelves.

"I'd really appreciate that, Amalia. Thank you," I said.

She nodded. "Let me make a call. I'll let you know what I find out."

I just about floated upstairs to the first stop on my cleaning routine, the master bedroom.

Jesus, if Amalia had more time these days, why the hell didn't she pick up her clothes off the floor? I started hanging the expensive designer dresses and jackets she'd thrown all over, when something black fluttered out of one of her pockets.

It was a condom, still in its wrapper.

Interesting.

"What's THAT?" Robbie yelled, climbing out from under his parents' bed.

Time to think quick.

"Robbie, don't you ever comb your hair?" I asked, reaching to run my fingers through his blond mop.

You'd think I'd come after the kid with a machete.

"GET OFF ME," he screamed, running out of the room.

Now I knew why his hair was never combed.

I tucked the condom into my blue jeans pocket and got back to work. I might not think much of Amalia, but I did want to be discreet.

She helps me, I help her. At least, that's the way I looked at it then.

CHAPTER 11

Thorn Quinton

I'd never seen anything like it.

At least not from the inside. Cal hadn't been kidding when he said these people lived like nothing either of us could ever imagine.

I rarely ventured to the Upper East Side. Why would I? There was nothing up there for me. I figure the last time I was in that part of town was when my brother was dealing, and I made a delivery for him to some rich fucker's place.

So it was weird I was up in this part of the city again for a completely different gig, one Cal had pulled me into.

A straight gig. My first, outside coaching the kids.

I had to hand it to the man. I don't know why he took a liking to me, but he showed me the way out of a shitty, dead end life, and had supported me every step of the way toward getting clean. I owed him—well, everything.

He believed in me when nobody else did. My brother and his cronies warned me I'd be back in their clutches in no time, begging for work, a fix, and their friendship. I don't know that I could have fought all that without the support of a friend like Cal.

So coming to work for him was a no-brainer. The fact that I might be well paid was just icing on the cake. I had nothing, I needed nothing, and I wanted nothing but a life lived honestly and consciously, as they'd taught us in rehab. So far, so good.

"You must be Thorn. I'm Stu," a bona fide New Yorker said with a friendly smile, clearly the cool doorman Cal went to Yankees games with.

"Nice to meet you, man," I said, extending my hand. "How'd you know my name?"

"Cal told me to expect you. He said you looked a little more… hip than most of the folks around here."

He laughed. Seemed like a nice guy. Must see all sorts of shit in a building like this.

"Where you from, man?" I asked.

"Bronx, baby. You?"

"Right here in Manhattan. Hell's Kitchen. From back in the day," I said.

He slapped his hand on his desk. "Holy shit. I remember the Kitchen from back in the day. What a place," he said, shaking his head and whistling.

Stu and I were going to get along fine.

I took a moment to look around the lobby of the building—the building where I'd be working for the von Malsen family. The marble floor shone like glass, and beautiful furniture was spread perfectly just like in a hotel lobby.

Beautiful furniture that was probably never sat on.

"Just look at this place," I said to Stu.

He raised his eyebrows. "I know, right. Blows the mind."

The elevator dinged, and when it opened, a woman in jeans and a hoodie with three dogs emerged, each pulling on their leash to see who could get outside first.

"Hey, Clare. Better not let those pups go on my shiny floor here," Stu said, bending to give the big one a scratch.

"Trying, Stu," she said as the dogs nearly pulled her arm off.

He turned back to me. "Dog walker. There are more people working for the folks in this building than there are actual folks living in the building."

Guess the more money you had, the more help you needed with your daily life.

Which didn't make a hell of a lot of sense.

"I'll catch ya later, Stu. Gotta head upstairs and get to work."

Stu nodded. "They're nice people, the von Malsens. You'll enjoy them."

"Thanks, man."

Well. I wasn't so sure I was going to enjoy the von Malsens, but I sure as hell would enjoy working with the lovely Lill.

Not that she'd been friendly, or even particularly nice for that matter. She was a working stiff just like the rest of us. But she seemed a little different. A lot of girls in New York were *on their way up*. That's how I put it. I didn't meet many of them, but occasionally I'd come across one who wanted to say she'd been with a genuine *rough guy* and dragged me home for a fuck.

It was a bit of a fetish for them, especially in a city like New York where the vast majority of men were buttoned up prepsters. Not to brag, but I was rarely in want of female company. It's just the way it was. Of course, these girls weren't about to take me home to Daddy, but they sure as hell wanted to suck my dick.

Who was I to say no?

"You must be Thorn," a pretty, petite woman said, opening the door.

She wore a sort of forced smile, and gave me the once over, settling on the neck tattoo that peeked out from the collar of my leather jacket.

"And you must be Mrs. von Malsen."

She laughed nervously.

Christ. She was one of *them*. Afraid of anyone who didn't look just like everybody else in her life. But I'd dealt with plenty of folks like that and always managed to win them over.

Footsteps clacked across the giant foyer and I looked to find Cal rushing our way. Christ, did he look conservative in his work duds of dress shoes, trousers, and a blazer with no tie. He probably fit perfectly in these parts.

He'd come a long way since he'd been on the force. And I'd come a long way since I was his informant.

"Thorn, good to see you. You've met Amalia?" he asked, looking between the two of us.

Amalia clasped her hands, not taking her eyes off Cal. "Oh yes."

I could swear there was adoration in her eyes. Did she have a thing for Cal? Now *that* could fuck things up for a guy.

"Let me show you around the house, Thorn," Cal said, gesturing toward a wide, curving stairway.

Holy shit. These people had stairs *in* their apartment.

We did a quick lap through the place, finishing up in the kitchen, where he showed me the back door that led to a stairwell.

And then Lill appeared, lugging a big basket of laundry.

Her hair was a little mussed and she was struggling with her load, but she was still the beauty I'd been thinking about since I'd met her.

"Oh, let me help you with that," I offered, reaching for the basket.

But she skirted around me. "Hey, Thorn. Amalia won't like that. But thank you anyway," she whispered.

Okay.

"Oh, Cal, may I have a word?" Amalia called.

He looked at me and smiled. "You don't mind chilling out here in the kitchen, do you? Be right back."

I took a seat at the kitchen counter and marveled at the sparkling whiteness of a kitchen that looked like no one had ever cooked a meal in, that's how spotless it was.

"I'm not sure about this arrangement," I overheard Amalia say in a quiet voice. "Thorn doesn't look the way a security person should."

Well, shit. I'd just arrived and already there were problems.

"Amalia, please stay open minded. Thorn is exactly what we need, especially right now."

She sighed. "All right. I guess it's all right. I know I can trust you, Cal. You're so good at what you do."

"Thank you, Amalia," he said, his footsteps indicating he was heading back to the kitchen.

"Don't listen to her," Lill said quietly. "She's pretty much an idiot."

I bit my tongue to keep from laughing.

"Dude, I heard what she said," I told Cal as soon as he joined us.

He waved his hand. "Ignore it. People like her can be that way."

Maybe I should have kept my moratorium in place on coming to the Upper East Side. I didn't need shit like this.

Cal read my expression. "Stick with me. Everything will work out fine. There's a lot at stake for these people. There are foreign operatives who think nothing of killing a diplomat's family."

Well. That put things into perspective.

"I'm taking Amalia to an event, where she'll be meeting her husband Eckie. I'll see you guys later," he said, and left.

I looked at Lill, folding laundry on the kitchen counter. She was cute as hell with her hair piled on top of her head so haphazardly that a good deal of it had fallen out of its clip and was now floating around her face.

Holy shit. This was going to be a problem.

So I excused myself to become more familiar with the house—and to get away from Lill.

"Who are *you*?"

I turned to find a five or six-year-old in a Superman cape with his hands on his hips, looking up at me with a scowl. Must be the infamous Robbie.

Jesus. With a tough little guy like this, I wasn't sure they needed a security detail.

"Oh. Hello. I'm Thorn."

He glared. "Are you another security man?"

I crouched down to his height. "I am. But it seems like you might not need me since you're Superman."

He held up a finger. "That's what I told my mom. But she doesn't listen."

"I suppose I could talk to her for you. Would that help?"

His face softened. "Yes, please. Talk to my mom for me."

The doorbell rang and Robbie went running for it.

"Hey, hold up little man. I have a feeling you know you're not supposed to open the door. That's a job for a grown-up."

He scrunched his face. "But I'm Superman!"

Jesus. This kid was a handful.

"It's just my nanny," he said.

I looked out the peephole, and it sure looked like a nanny waiting in the hallway.

"All right. Go ahead," I said.

He yanked the door open. "Hi, Rose," he said.

"Robbie, hey there," she said, smiling at me and setting her things down. "How 'bout a hug, buddy?"

He crossed his arms again. "No. I'm Superman. I don't give hugs."

They retreated into the recesses of the house, bickering all the way.

In another hour, Lill was done with her work, and grabbed her jacket and bag from the laundry room.

"Ready?" she said.

When we got into the elevator, she yawned. "Excuse me. I'm so tired. I guess cleaning houses will do that. What about you? What were you doing before Cal roped you into his gig?"

Waiting to meet her, obviously.

"Coaching kids' basketball. But now that I'm here, I'll just do it on a volunteer basis."

She looked surprised. "That's so cool."

"So. Where to?" I asked as we waved goodnight to Stu.

"I'm going home. Well, to my friend Beebie's anyway. I'm so tired I'm going straight to bed."

"Okay. Well, my bike is just right over here," I said, pointing in its direction.

"Oh my god, you have a motorcycle. I love motorcycles," she exclaimed.

Shit. A woman who loved bikes. One of my weaknesses.

"Here's your helmet," I said, pulling my extra one out from under the seat.

She fumbled with it for a moment.

"Here. Let me."

I reached for her chin strap and wove it through the buckle, taking care to push her hair out of the way.

And Christ, did she smell good. It was nothing fancy, maybe just some hand lotion or something, but it grabbed me by the balls and didn't let go.

When we got going, I drove more slowly than usual since I was riding a passenger, which is probably why the car that had followed us for several blocks was so close. I'd noticed it right off the bat—it's not easy to tail a motorcycle with the nimble way we can negotiate traffic. Lill was oblivious, fortunately, just enjoying the ride.

Jesus. Cal hadn't been kidding about these people. Whoever the hell *they* were. I was glad Lill was in my hands, where I knew she'd be safe. And the people back there trailing us? I didn't care if they worked for the fucking Israeli Mossad, they'd never dealt with the likes of me. I came up on these New York streets and had access to a few more secrets than they did, of that I was sure.

After I'd led them on a nice little sightseeing tour of Manhattan, it was time to step things up and lose the fuckers. But first I'd make them earn their pay.

"Lill," I called over my shoulder.

"Yeah?"

"I'm going to pick up the pace since you seem comfortable. Hang on, okay?"

It was as good a lie as any.

"Okay. Let's go!" she yelled, pumping her fist in the air.

Before I poured on the speed, I discreetly reached down to my right ankle to touch my loaded gun. I hoped to hell I wouldn't need to use it, but if I did, I was ready. Then, I brushed my hand over Lill's to make sure her arms were wrapped tight around my waist. She gripped me tighter.

Smart girl.

That's when I opened the throttle, and in second gear screeched ahead of all the traffic surrounding us. After a few blocks and a couple random turns, I'd lost our trail.

But they'd be back. It was just a matter of time.

"Here we are," I said when we'd arrived at Lill's friend's house. "Hope you had fun."

I knew I sure had. It wasn't every day that a man got to ride a beautiful passenger *and* outrun bad guys.

I turned off the bike and packed away her helmet after she'd shaken her crazy red hair out of it.

Fuck, I was dying to touch it.

But I didn't.

She smiled at me. "That was fun. Just what I needed after a crummy day. Thank you. And thanks for the ride home. I probably would have been okay in a cab, though. But no more subway, right?" She laughed.

I wasn't sure how much to tell her, so I kept my mouth shut. She still didn't seem to understand the gravity of the threat against her. Maybe it was just as well.

I was walking her to the door when she turned to me. "By the way, ignore that Amalia. She really is horrible sometimes. It's so funny. She has everything in the world, and yet she can't manage to be a nice person."

She shook her head sadly.

"Yeah, I kind of figured that out," I said, shrugging. "Not my problem, is how I look at it."

No, I was more interested in the 'problem' standing right in front of me.

CHAPTER 12

Lill

I waited as Thorn started his bike back up and peeled out onto the street. I even waited until the roar of the engine was too faint to hear before I pressed the elevator's *up* button.

I needed to make sure he wasn't getting some crazy sort of idea about hanging around for surveillance. I mean, I appreciated everyone's efforts and all, but Amalia sort of had a point. No one was going to bother with me. I was just a tiny cog in a big wheel of important people. I didn't see how I could be worth anyone's time.

Although I had helped a forensic artist put together a sketch of the guys who'd tried to grab Robbie. So if they were trying to stop me from doing that, well, too late.

"Hey, Beebs!" I called, running straight for my room.

"There you are. Hurry up and get ready."

I tore off my clothes and ran to the bathroom to wash up and apply new makeup. I re-shaped my hair, partially crushed by Thorn's helmet, and used a little hairspray to keep it under control.

"You need to wear nicer underwear," Beebie said, turning her nose up at my GAP cotton panties.

"Really? We're gonna worry about that now? Besides, no one's going to see my panties tonight."

She rolled her eyes. "Well, wear that push-up bra I gave you. It will make the dress fall better."

Jesus Christ. I whipped off the old bra I was wearing and dug out the push-up. I poured my boobs into it and stepped into my Little Black Dress.

"Zip me, please," I said, jumping in front of Beebie.

I reached for the shoes I was wearing, hand-me-downs from her, and was ready to go.

"I can't believe you got ready that fast. You look amazing," she said.

I could swear there was a tear in her eye.

"Did you call the Uber?" I asked.

She looked at her phone. "Yup. They're pulling up right now."

"Okay. Let's go," I said.

I couldn't say the recent events with the von

Malsens and their growing security team hadn't had any effect on me whatsoever—when we exited Beebie's building I scanned the street as far as I could see, and took a good look at the Uber driver after checking to make sure his license plate matched what the app was telling us.

Once we were at the party, everything would be fine. It would be crowded and fun, and no one would ever think to look for me there.

Especially not Cal, Dex, and Thorn.

Not that they'd ever know I went out without notifying them. That would remain my secret. If they found out, well, it wouldn't be pretty.

"This place is crawling with people from publishing," I told Beebie as soon as we had glasses of champagne in our hands.

"Well, you tear it up, girl. Don't worry about me. I'll just be cruising for rich, good-looking men. And of course, people who need their homes decorated."

She was so awesome. She always came with me to events like this, and half the time she dressed me, too.

Beebie and I had met in yoga. She was always in the front row wearing those expensive Lululemon outfits, and could do the perfect handstand. The bitch didn't even wobble. I, on the other hand, usually hid in the back in my crappy Target yoga pants and tank top, and could only barely do a handstand if I leaned against the wall.

One day in class I yelled at a guy who wouldn't stop

MIKA LANE

staring at my crotch. The class came to a halt and the instructor, in her yoga-voice, asked if there was a problem. The guy grabbed his mat and left, and the teacher returned to our sequence of poses.

You never know what kind of fucking weirdos you're going to meet in New York.

But after that, half the class buzzed around me like I was some kind of superhero. Seemed crotch guy had been coming to yoga for the sole purpose of picking up chicks for a while.

Beebie was especially impressed with my outburst and we became fast friends, even though she was a glamorous interior designer, and I was a struggling writer. She didn't care about status-y stuff like that. She liked a woman who had some guts and who was going for what she wanted.

Beebie took off through the crowded party in search of men and clients, and I began to wander as if I were looking for someone I knew. In reality, I knew who I wanted to talk to and make an impression on, but first I needed to meet them.

After all, that's why I was there.

To make contacts without coming across as a stalker. A delicate balance I hoped my expensive dress would help achieve.

"Lill!" a voice called from across the room.

Shit.

"Hey, Bert," I said as he bounded to my side.

My heart sank. No way could I do the reconnaissance I needed with Bert as my uninvited wingman.

"That's quite a dress there, Lill. I approve," he said, looking me up and down.

Like I gave a shit.

But Bert was part of my writing class, and he knew a lot of people. I was in no position to give him the same treatment I did the guy in my yoga class.

He shouldered up to me. "Lotsa heavy hitters here, Lill. You going to talk to any of them?"

That was my plan, idiot.

But I took a deep breath.

"Oh, I don't know. Hey, do you know anybody here?" I asked with wide eyes.

He held his head up and sniffed. "I do. I sure do." He scanned the party as if it had been thrown for him.

Douche.

"Do you know anyone here from Beauté?"

He rolled his eyes, just like I knew he would. "Really? You want to meet people at a fashion magazine?"

"Bert, it's not just fashion, it's women's—"

He waved away my protest. "Whatever. I can't expect everyone to have the same ambitions I do."

Speaking of which.

"What does that mean? What are your plans?" I asked.

"I'm going to be the next James Michener. You know, write historical novels."

Um, yeah.

"James Michener was an educator, you know. What kind of experience do you have with that?"

He gave me a dirty look. "That is a surmountable challenge."

Beebie came bounding toward us, turning heads as she always did in her slinky silk halter top and wide-legged pants.

"This is my friend from class, Bert," I said. "Bert, Beebie."

Beebie brushed a piece of her platinum pixie hair behind her ear, and broke into her oversized smile. "Hello. I'm Beebie."

I wished I'd had the time to warn her that he was not worth it.

"Beebie. What a charming name," Bert hummed.

"So you guys are in class together. How fun," she said, gazing directly at me.

Yeah, she wanted info. Some sort of message. But Bert was watching too closely.

"What kind of writing do you do, Beebie?" he asked, charmed by her as all men were.

She dropped her head back and laughed. "Oh, I don't write."

Bert frowned. "You don't?" He looked at me as if to confirm. "Why are you here then?"

Oh my god.

Beebie's eyes widened at his lack of tact, but it didn't set her back. "Same reason everybody is. To have fun." She raised her glass toward mine and we clinked.

"Well, what do you do, then?" he asked.

Ugh. Such a New York question.

Beebie scanned the room, by now clued into Bert's dickishness, looking for an escape.

"I'm a designer. Interior designer."

Bert scoffed.

Big mistake.

"So, like you pick out couches and paint walls? Stuff like that?" he asked.

Beebie looked at him blankly. "Yeah. That's exactly what I do."

And she walked off, disappearing into the crowd.

He turned back to me. Because, of course.

"So, what are you working on now?" he asked.

"I'm finishing my second romance novel. You know, I read a piece of it in class a couple weeks ago?"

He sighed. "Right. Hey, listen, don't you want to work on something more... literary?"

And here we go.

"I like what I'm working on, Bert," I barked, a little more loudly than I meant to.

He put an arm around my shoulders and pulled me close. "Of course you do, Lill. Don't get upset. Now tell me, when are we going out? Like on a real date?"

Shit. I should have known this was coming.

I inched out from under his arm, desperately holding on to my smile. "Oh, I don't see that in the cards for us, Bert. But being friends is great."

As if that would take care of it.

Wishful thinking.

He cleared his throat, then looked down at his feet, shaking his head. When he looked back up at me, his eyes were dark. Scary dark. "Look Lill. You are a cleaning lady. Who wants to write—"

"I *do* write, Bert. I write romance novels."

He waved away my words. "Do you really think" — he paused and looked around the party— "that you can afford to be so picky?"

Oh no he didn't.

I waved Beebie over, who fortunately hadn't wandered far. It was time to take a stand.

"Beebie," I said.

"Hey, guys." She looked from one of us to the other.

"Bert just said I should go out with him because, as a cleaning lady who wants to write, I mustn't have many other options."

Beebie's head snapped back on its axis and her eyes narrowed. "Oh, Lill," she said like a sports announcer, "Bert just said that because he has a small dick."

His mouth dropped open. That's all he had.

I tried to hold back my amusement, but it escaped like a large horselaugh. Not very ladylike, but it was the best I could do in the situation.

And all eyes turned in our direction. But only for a moment. Then everyone went back to their ass-kissing.

"C'mon," Beebie said, grabbing my arm. "We have some mixing to do."

CHAPTER 13

Lill

"Morning, Amalia," I said the next day, unable to muster my usual smile.

I was in a shit mood from the stupid party the night before. And mad at myself for spending so much on a dress that did me absolutely no good.

"Hi, Lill," she said, smiling sweetly.

Warning, warning.

"Eckie and I are having a few friends over tonight for drinks. Would you be interested in sticking around and serving, cleaning up, that sort of thing?"

I just looked at her blankly. I didn't know what to say.

Which probably made her realize she needed to sweeten the pot.

"I'll pay you double your normal rate, and make sure you get a ride home with one of the security guys."

Oh, why the fuck not? It's not like I needed to rush home and work on my book since my writing was so mundane anyway.

"Sure, I'm happy to help. It sounds like fun," I lied.

She squeezed her fists together and jumped a little. "Oh, super. Thank you Lill."

"Hey, Amalia?" I asked.

She'd been running off but turned back to me. "Yes?"

"Um, have you read my book yet? The one I emailed you?"

Confusion crossed her face.

Bitch didn't even remember she'd asked to read my romance novel.

But then she nodded frantically. "Oh my gosh, right. I haven't yet. But I plan to, soon."

Fuck. Why did I send her my book? I didn't want her looking at anything of mine.

What a mistake.

The von Malsens' party was mellow, with about a dozen or so attractive, fit people having wine and cocktails and discussing things like the condition of the New York streets, and which museum they were giving money to this season.

"Can I take that empty glass from you, Mr. von Malsen?"

"Lill. I told you. Call me Eckie. Say, Tom, have you met the newest member of our staff, Lill?"

Tom took a step back to see me from head to toe because, obviously, he was a total creep, and turned back to Eckie.

"You know, Eck, staff are getting better and better looking every year. You'd better watch it, or I'll try to steal Lill right from under your nose."

Just as Eckie dropped his head back to laugh, Tom put a hand on my shoulder, which quickly migrated down to my ass, where he took a generous squeeze.

Really? Men still did that?

I scowled at him and squirmed out of his reach.

"Amalia," I said, hanging up my apron in the pantry, "I think you're all set for the night. I'll head out now."

I considered telling her how Tom had helped himself to my ass cheek, but decided to save it for another time.

Dex drove me home in silence. I was more disgusted than ever with my lame-ass life, and more determined than ever to become an ex-cleaning lady.

I was going to send out as many resumes as I could find places to send them to, even if it kept me up all night long.

CHAPTER 14

Cal

I was glad Thorn hadn't told Lill about the car that had followed them home that night when they were on the motorcycle. Not that I wanted her to be in the dark about what she was up against, but I didn't want her getting spooked to the point of freaking out.

I'd seen that before with clients.

As it was, she seemed to be taking everything going on around her in stride, keeping her head down and letting us protect her the best we could.

Thank goodness. I'd hate to see her be careless. That could put her, and the entire operation, in jeopardy.

Of course, I'd generally hate to see anything happen

to her, anyway. I was developing a real taste for her sassy, suffer-no-fools approach to life.

It didn't hurt that she was a stunning redhead, either.

The sad part was, I didn't think she'd be in my life for long. I knew her type, and for someone like her, working for a self-centered twit like Amalia was tolerable for only so long. Something would happen that would cause her to blow her top, and that would be her last day of employment at the von Malsens.

It was a shame, because Eckie was a solid guy. How he'd ended up with his wife, I'd never understand.

But for the time Lill was around, I planned to get to know her as well as I could. And I knew the other guys felt the same.

Which was fine with me. I wasn't the jealous type. Well, I wasn't the super-jealous type.

Since we guys—my newly formed security team—were still getting a sense of what we were up against, Dex had wisely suggested we send Lill out for some 'errands' and see what sort of attention she attracted. We'd watch from a close distance to see if anyone tried to get close to her.

"I'm ready to run out for Amalia now," she told me, pulling on her jacket.

She pulled her long hair out of the collar, and while it swung down her back, I got a whiff of her shampoo.

Fuck if I wasn't dying to burying my face in that hair.

And other places.

"Okay. Just like we said, do your thing, and I'll be watching. You might not be able to see me at all times, but I'll be close. If you need anything just holler and I'll be there."

She shrugged. "Sure. Whatever floats your boat."

Jesus, what a smart ass.

I loved it.

Lill set out for her errands, or her 'bitch chores' as she called them, walking briskly like any other New York girl. She took long strides, swung her arms widely, and let her wild hair whip around her head. She jaywalked a couple times, looking both ways and jogging across the street in her black Converse Chucks.

If I didn't know better, I could swear she was trying to lose me.

But she wouldn't do that.

Would she?

Yeah, she was making it difficult for me to tail her. She was a pain that way. But when she turned a corner and was out of sight for a moment, I started to get a little nervous. I ran the length of the block, and as soon as I rounded the same corner, I saw her talking to some guy.

Actually he was talking to *her*. Or trying to.

I took a seat on someone's stoop just a few feet away, and pretended to scroll through my phone.

I also felt for the gun on my right hip. Just in case.

"Hey, I've seen you around the neighborhood. What's your name?" he asked her.

She stuffed her hands in her pockets and kept walking. "Sorry. Not in the mood."

That's when he reached for her arm and yanked her to a stop.

"What the—"

He got in her face. "I was being friendly. You don't have to be such a—"

But his speech came to an abrupt stop. A gun poking in your ribs will do that.

He looked at me. "What the fuck man? I was just trying to talk to this snotty bitch here—"

It was my turn to grab his arm.

Lill stood there, her eyes wide at the sight of my gun.

"She said *no thanks*. Now you can be a gentleman and walk away with your tail between your legs, or I can beat the shit out of you so you have to crawl away."

The smug look on his face was replaced by fright. He dropped her arm.

"Apologize to the lady," I demanded

He turned to look at her. "Sorry," he mumbled.

I released him with a little shove.

He hustled down the street, slowing only once to look back over his shoulder.

"Holy crap," Lill breathed. "That was… something."

I put my gun away. "Are you okay?"

She watched the guy turn a corner. "Yeah. I'm fine."

"He was mostly harmless, fortunately for you, unfortunately for him. The reason I stepped up, though, was that I didn't initially know whether or not he was some douchebag trying to pick you up, or if he was actually trouble."

I couldn't blame the guy for trying with Lill. She was a head-turner and I'd bet crap like that happened to her all the time. But this guy took it too far with the arm grabbing and name-calling.

Had he learned a lesson? I hoped so. I sure as hell was glad I was there.

Lill's surprise turned into amusement. "It was pretty funny. Did you see his face? I wouldn't be surprised if he wet his pants."

"You're right. It was kind of funny. There he was, thinking he might talk to a pretty girl, and he gets a gun shoved in his ribs and is forced to apologize."

She put her hand over her mouth to hide her giggles, and in a moment, she had me laughing, too.

"You know, Lill, you should smile more."

She rolled her eyes at me.

"Fine. Be a smart ass. But you're so fucking pretty."

She play-punched me in the arm. "Now you're the one trying to get into my panties."

She had no idea.

CHAPTER 15

Cal

Aside from the failed pick-up-artist, tailing Lill on her errands didn't produce any other surprises.

"What do you like to write?" I asked when we were back at the von Malsens, where she was folding freshly washed sheets. She shook the wrinkles out of the expensive white cotton and somehow managed to get them into tidy compact squares, almost like when they were brand new out of the package.

"I like to do all different kinds of writing. Personal essays, newsy stuff for blog posts, things like that. But my favorite is romance."

I didn't see Lill as the romantic type, cynical as she was. But maybe there was more to her than met the eye. Which intrigued me.

"Are you writing a story now?" I asked.

She looked at me coyly. "I might be."

Oh shit. Was she writing about bodyguards?

No. There was nothing interesting about bodyguards.

She gathered all the folded sheets into a basket. "I know it's probably hard to imagine, but I really do believe in romance. It makes me happy."

High heels clicked into the kitchen and we both turned to see Amalia, perfectly coifed as usual. She looked between the two of us like we were bad little kids.

I loved my job, but that woman could be unbearable.

She scowled at Lill, but when she looked up at me, she smiled like she always did. "Cal, can you do me a favor and go down to the lobby and bring up our grocery delivery?"

Oh. Right. She was bent out of shape that I was talking to Lill.

So petty. And so predictable.

"Sure, Amalia. Happy to."

She clicked her nails on the marble kitchen counter. "Super. Thanks."

Then she turned to Lill, eyebrows raised.

"I'm running these sheets upstairs," she said.

Amalia just nodded as Lill made herself scarce.

"Hey, Stu," I said when I got down to the lobby. "I'm here for the von Malsens' groceries."

He reached behind the front desk and handed me a couple bags. "Doesn't Lill usually come down for this stuff?"

I nodded. "Usually. But I'm pretty sure Amalia was sending me a message in asking me to come down. She... doesn't like it when I talk to Lill."

Stu rolled his eyes and lowered his voice. "It's funny. She's beautiful and yet she's jealous of one of her staff."

I didn't get it, either.

I let myself back into the von Malsens' with my key and headed for the kitchen. But before I reached it, I overheard muffled talking coming from the library.

I wasn't normally one to eavesdrop—my clients could do whatever the hell they wanted—but given the circumstances, my curiosity was piqued.

"Well, you'll have to try again. Yes, yes, I know. I miss you too. I need to run. Eckie will be home soon," Amalia said.

Oh shit.

That didn't sound good.

"Oh my god, that woman is maddening," Lill wailed as soon as we were in my Jeep, driving her home. "How do you deal with her?"

"I keep my focus on Eckie. He's a great guy. Unfortunately, you don't get to spend as much time with him as I do. You're stuck with Amalia."

I'd find that hard to take, too.

"How long are you going to work there? For the von Malsens?" I asked.

To be honest, I didn't know how she'd lasted as long as she had.

She leaned her forehead against the window. "Well, I've been sending resumes to magazines. And trying to get my book published. But if something doesn't happen soon, I may need to take on another cleaning client."

I pulled up in front of her friend's building. "Well, you could always clean for me."

She dropped her head back and laughed. "Yeah, right. God knows what I'd find. Would your pockets be full of condoms too?"

I looked at her. "Why do you say that?"

She studied me for a moment. "I probably shouldn't have said anything, but when I was picking up Amalia's clothes the other day, a condom fell out of her pocket."

Interesting.

"Did you say anything?" I asked.

"Oh hell no. I actually just stuck it in my own

pocket before it was discovered and caused god knows what kind of trouble."

I suppose it could have been hers and Eckie's. But he'd confided in me awhile back that they couldn't have any more kids and that they were lucky to have Robbie.

"Let me walk you in," I said.

When we reached the front door, she used her card key to get inside. Instead of stopping there, and saying goodnight, I followed her further.

She raised an eyebrow. "And where are you going?" she asked with a laugh.

I reached for her hand and pulled her past the front desk guy, and to a small corridor I'd spotted behind the elevators when I'd scoped the place out.

"What are you doing?" she asked breathlessly.

Silly question.

I backed her up against a wall, kissing her temple, then her cheek, and moving down to her neck.

She sighed and her eyes fell closed.

I buried my fingers in her lush hair and pulled her to me until our lips met. I kissed her softly at first and then with the urgency that had been building inside me almost since the first time we'd met.

"Mmmm," I murmured, taking a step back to admire her freckles. "So pretty," I said.

She blushed. She actually fucking blushed.

"C'mon," I said, leading her toward the elevators. "We both have early mornings."

I kissed her one more time and as I started to walk

away, I realized she wasn't releasing my fingers. So I brought her hand to my lips and kissed it too.

"Good night," I said, and headed out.

I looked over my shoulder one last time and there my lovely girl stood, running a finger over her lips, smiling.

CHAPTER 16

Lill

"Ohmygod Beebs. You won't believe what I just did."

She turned to me from her overstuffed sofa, where she had her feet on the coffee table and was watching an old *Sex And The City.* She was sipping a Cosmo like she always did when she watched it.

"What? What'd you do?"

I plopped down next to her and kicked my shoes off. "I kissed one of those security guard guys. Who I work with at the von Malsens."

She slapped my leg. "Well, you little ho bag. Which one?"

"The super tall one. The one I was pissed at who felt me up on my first day. Cal."

She put the TV on pause and sighed. "He wasn't feeling you up. C'mon, don't be a drama queen. He was doing his job."

Yeah, he was. And his job was feeling me up.

I loved Beebie but it chafed me when she didn't take my side. I couldn't help it. "They didn't do that to you when you went over the first time, did they?"

"Well, no. But I'd been going over to their place for a couple years before they even had security. So I guess Amalia felt like she knew me."

What Amalia knew was that Beebie was of *her world*. A cleaning person like me *was not*. She was elitist, plain and simple.

I wanted to count the days until I could give Amalia my notice that I was moving on to something new that would be both prestigious and impressive. People like her hated when someone like me succeeded or got ahead in the world. But I'd show her I could do more than pick up her dirty clothes off the floor. And hide her cheating-ass condoms.

But I didn't dare start counting. Not yet. Because there was no end in sight. I was trying, though. In fact I'd sent a shit load of resumes just the night before.

And then there was the agent Amalia offered to introduce me to. But I doubted anything would come of that. She was the type of person who wanted to get your hopes up and then took pleasure in seeing them dashed.

Someday soon, people like that would have no power over me. None at all.

But until then, I was her cleaning wench. And it pretty much sucked.

The only saving grace was the freaking gorgeous security team working for her. The same guys she drooled over whenever they were in her house.

"Hey, Beebs, what's with Amalia, anyway? I have a feeling she and Eckie are not as solid as they pretend to be."

She pursed her lips. "Well. Keep this to yourself. But word has it she married Eckie for his money and status."

Well, duh. It didn't take a brain surgeon to figure that out. But enough about the von Malsens. They weren't my problem, only my employer. Temporary employer.

"Hey, speaking of the security team, did they ever find out we sneaked out to that party the other night?" she asked.

"Oh, god no. That would be a shit show of epic proportion if they did. We gotta keep that mum."

She pretended to twist a key in front of her lips. "I'm not telling anyone. Although if they are as hot as you say they are, I don't know why you don't invite them around. Could be fun," she said with a twinkle in her eyes.

It would most definitely be fun.

I texted Cal the next morning that I would catch an Uber to the von Malsens. I wanted to get there early so I could leave early for writing class. It was strange to check in with him about my comings and goings and my mode of transportation, but I figured I'd keep the peace for the time being.

He really did seem like a nice guy, if a little overbearing.

And his being hot as hell certainly made it easier to put up with. Well, that and the fact that his kiss just about melted me.

Every time I looked at him from now on, it would be all I could think about. I just knew it. So, I planned to look at him as little as possible.

It was just a one-time fluke, anyway. What would a guy like him want with a cleaning lady, anyway?

So when I arrived at work that morning in my Uber, and spotted Cal out front chatting with a beautiful blonde, I didn't give a shit.

Yeah, right.

I hopped out of the car and with my head down, headed straight for the door.

"Morning, Lill," he called. "Hey, Dex is working today. Just wanted to let you know."

I just waved hello and dashed inside.

Fuck that guy. Fuck all of them.

"Hey, Lill," Dex said when I got to the apartment. "I'm taking Amalia out in a bit."

Her heels clicked across the floor toward me as she pulled a long trench coat on. "Robbie's still sleeping."

Once again, I was a substitute nanny.

"Okay. I'll see you later, then," I said, heading to the kitchen to drop my stuff.

The house was eerily silent after they left. Not that the place was ever noisy, but without any sound or movement, it seemed almost sterile. Museum-like. A strange contrast to the cacophony that was the street below.

I pulled open the terrace doors for quick proof that the city was alive and well. I was instantly reassured that it was still humming, despite the hermetically sealed home the von Malsens had crafted for themselves. I missed my own apartment, though, the one I'd not been back to since I'd found it ransacked, and where I'd taken for granted the consistent hum of street noise. After getting used to it, I'd come to find it comforting. With it, I never felt lonely. It reminded me of how alive I was.

Beebie's apartment was quieter than mine, but not as sound-proof as this place. Along with a better view and more upscale neighbors, it seemed like money could also buy quiet, something hard to come by in a place like Manhattan.

I checked out the street below where more than half

the traffic was yellow cabs endlessly picking up and discharging passengers. Cal and the woman he'd been speaking to were long gone, probably to someplace private where he could kiss her like he had me just the day before. Asshole.

Without Amalia's or anybody's else's interference, I finished my morning cleaning and set up my laptop in the kitchen to do a little writing before Robbie woke up and destroyed the peace.

I couldn't deny that my story ideas of late had been influenced by the hot security dudes who were now a part of my daily life. Their vigilance might have been inconvenient, but they sure as hell were something to look at—and something to fantasize about.

In fact, just the night before, I had to admit I'd been a little hot and bothered by Cal's kiss. I couldn't lie. I'd liked it. A lot. And I wanted it to happen again.

Against my better judgment. But fuck that.

After I'd said goodnight to Beebie that night, who was still on her SATC binge, I crawled under my fluffy down comforter and reached my hand into my PJ bottoms. Stroking my folds, I'd grown increasingly wet as I thought about all the dirty things the guys might do to me.

I was such a perv.

First, I imagined being ravished by Thorn. He was so coarse, with his unwavering gaze, leathered skin, and long scar. He grabbed me by my hair, yanking my head down to his cock, which he'd whipped out of his jeans and held like it was a fucking rocket.

With his free hand, he'd rubbed a rough thumb over my lower lip until my mouth opened. He pushed that thumb inside, pulling my jaw down as he aimed himself inside me. Removing his thumb, he pushed himself to the back of my throat until I gagged and my eyes watered, streaming black mascara down my cheeks.

While I sucked him, Dex reached into my panties and spread my wet excitement from my clit to ass. I arched back against him, begging for more contact as he slipped one finger inside me, followed by another.

And Cal sat off to the side, his eyes half-closed and his smile crooked, stroking the cock that he'd pulled out of his pants.

I was surrounded by three of the most gorgeous, strong, and brave men I'd ever known. It was exhilarating.

As was the orgasm I brought myself.

I'd slept well that night.

And now I wanted more.

My fantasies of late were turning into great fodder for my second romance novel. I'd considered reading the sexy scenes to my writing group, but I didn't want to be responsible for giving any of those prudes heart attacks. So, I figured I'd try them out on Beebie.

I got a good few pages done on my latest story when I heard a key in the von Malsens' front door. I folded up my laptop and tucked it away before I went to see who it was.

"Hi, Lill," Eckie said. "I came home for lunch. Is Robbie up yet?"

It was such a pleasure to see Eckie. He was so nice.

"I was just about to go up and get him." I headed for the stairs.

"Amalia," he called.

"She's out. Dex took her somewhere."

Confusion crossed his face. "She is? Where'd she go?"

Did he really think she told me anything more than what needed cleaning in their house?

"I'm not sure, Eckie. I'll go get Robbie."

By the time I came back downstairs, Dex had returned.

"Hey Dex, where'd you drop Amalia? Eckie's looking for her."

"I dropped her at the public library for a luncheon. I'll pick her up in an hour and a half."

Eckie reached for his phone. "You didn't stay with her?" he asked.

Dex shook his head. "She said the event had security."

"Okay. Interesting. She's not picking up," Eckie said.

I wanted no part of what was or was not about to happen, so I dragged Robbie to the kitchen for his lunch.

But Eckie wanted lunch too, and was right on my

heels when his phone rang. He took it out to the living room.

"Amalia? I was worried. I didn't know you'd be out. What? Okay. Fine. I'll see you then."

He returned to the kitchen. "She had her phone turned off," he said, settling onto a stool at the counter to have lunch with his little boy.

Yeah. Phone turned off, my ass.

CHAPTER 17

Lill

Dex had the honor of driving me home that night after the night nanny—the *real* nanny, as Amalia called her—arrived.

"Hey, do you mind if we stop at this corner store? I'd love to get a cheap bottle of white wine."

Dex steered his car over to the curb and turned on his flashers. "You like cheap white? Now, I would not have taken you for a girl who liked cheap anything."

He flashed me his devastating smile.

The bastard.

I knew who I'd be writing about that night.

"It's a weakness of mine," I replied with a smile.

Give him something to chew on.

He got out of the car with me, waiting at the shop's entrance as I hustled in to make my purchase.

I always wondered how corner stores, with their odd mish-mash of goods, managed to stay open. Sure, everything they carried was marked way up in the name of convenience, but they always seemed just sleepy enough to make me wonder how much stuff they actually sold.

I crouched to check out the lesser wines, tucked onto the lower store shelves where you really had to look if you wanted a bargain, and scooted in closer to let another customer pass behind me down the narrow aisle. I pulled out something that looked decent for its ten-dollar price, and blew at the dust that had collected on the bottle's neck.

"That looks like a good one," the deep-voiced customer said.

I stood back up, squinting to read the wine's label, when something shiny caught my eye.

I looked over at the customer, who was holding a gun.

Pointed at me.

What. The. Fuck.

"Don't say a word. Come with me," he said.

I glanced toward the door, where Dex leaned, scrolling through his phone, and the check out counter, where the clerk paged through the day's newspaper.

All, unaware of my situation.

"Don't make a sound," the man growled quietly, taking me by the upper arm.

Fuck all. Guess the guys hadn't been exaggerating when they'd suspected someone was after my ass. And now here I was, confronted with the danger I'd been poo-pooing all along.

"C'mon. We'll go out the back door," he said quietly, his eyes scanning back and forth.

But my would-be captor was not as smart as either of us thought, fortunately for me, because I sure as hell didn't have any ideas about how to out-maneuver him. With a tug on my arm, he pulled me slightly off balance. The bottle of cheap white wine I'd pulled from the bottom shelf?

It crashed to the ground, grabbing the attention of both the counter clerk and Dex, who was on us in a second.

Dex must have moved like lightning because in seconds he appeared from the other end of the aisle, running up behind my would-be abductor and striking him on the temple with the butt of his gun. The guy stumbled, knocking several wine bottles onto the floor, and sank to his knees.

"Lill, run," Dex yelled, grabbing my hand and pulling me out of the store.

On the way out, I glanced at the clerk, whose eyes were wide as he reached under the counter and retrieved his own gun.

Jesus. Did everyone have a gun except for me?

"Get in," he barked, jumping behind the wheel and taking off before I'd even closed my door.

I sank down in my seat and held on as Dex tore through traffic.

After bursting through more red lights than I wanted to count and turning several corners, Dex pulled over on a quiet street, using all the car's mirrors to keep an eye on everything around us.

"Are you okay? What happened?" he asked, breathing hard.

"I... um... I don't know. It happened so fast," I mumbled.

He reached for my hand. "Lill. Are you okay?"

I looked over at him. "I... I think so."

But I wasn't so sure. My smug idea about where I fit in the world had been turned fully upside down. I was utterly vulnerable. And when it came down to it, I was pretty damn weak with little or no ability defend myself. All I could do was count on the security guys the von Malsens were paying to look out for me.

The fucking von Malsens. I would not be in this position, or anything like it, if it weren't for whatever bullshit they had going on in their lives. When I had the chance, and at the appropriate time, I planned to give them a very big piece of my mind, and thank them for foisting their fucked up lives on me.

"I can't believe that just happened. Where did he come from? What was he going to do to me? What if you hadn't been there?"

Dex squeezed my hand. "I don't blame you for being upset, sweetie. It's completely natural. I'm calling the guys and taking you to my place. You'll be safer there, at least for the night."

I just looked straight ahead, too out of it to suggest any alternatives. There were no alternatives, at least that I knew of, to following Dex's suggestion. If he said I was going over to his place, that's where I was going.

CHAPTER 18

Dex

Lill dialed her roommate from the car. "Hey, Beebs, it's me. I'm staying at one of the security guy's places tonight. I'll tell you more later, but don't expect me home. Love ya."

I felt for Lill. I really did. She'd gotten the scare of a lifetime, and would feel unsteady for some time to come. Anyone having gone through what she had would feel the same, but she'd been somewhat in denial about it all, so what had happened in the convenience store was a doubly hard blow. To have everything you believe about your safety in this world proven wrong in a matter of seconds would fuck up even the strongest person.

"So this is where you live," she said, looking around the lobby of the ultra modern building. I'd bought into it when I'd decided to settle in New York with my private security job payout.

Yeah, my line of work had been that lucrative.

Well, my old line of work. Which I'd picked up again, but only for the short term.

Yeah, keep telling yourself that, asshole.

To gain entrance, I pressed a pass code to open the huge metal front door to my building, which permitted us into a lobby of soaring concrete walls. It was sort of prison-like, but after I'd gotten used to it, I found its simplicity soothing. The homeowner's association every now and then discussed getting furniture for the lobby, but we always walked away with the same conclusion. No one would sit on it, so why spend the dough?

Another, unique to me, code got us access to the elevator that took us to my floor. One of the best features of the building was that when an elevator was on route, it would stop on no other floors. No picking up extra passengers until it was their turn to use the elevator, when they'd have it all to themselves.

People like me are attracted to buildings like this.

The elevator let us out into a small hallway facing my door, which opened when I pressed my thumb on it. I turned the lever, and we were inside my place, safe and sound.

When you've done the work I used to do, you spend

the rest of your life looking over your shoulder. There would never be a time when I was one hundred percent safe. Because of that, I did all I could to lessen risk. That was how I ended up living in a fortress. An impenetrable, urban fortress.

"Jesus. Look at this view," Lill breathed.

I wasn't on the building's top floor, but I could still see over a few of the surrounding buildings and enjoyed a decent view of the city. I had no complaints and in fact felt pretty fucking lucky to have landed the place I had.

"Want a burger?" I asked Lill.

She pulled up a stool to my kitchen counter. "Yes, that sounds awesome. I'm actually starving now that I think of it."

Terror can do that to you.

"Beer?" I asked.

She nodded her head enthusiastically.

"Hey, so you know Cal from college?"

It dawned on me how little time I'd had to chat with her up till now. She knew practically nothing about me, and what I knew about her, I'd pretty much learned from Cal.

"Sure did."

She took a draw on her beer and closed her eyes as she swallowed. "Oh my god, this is so good. So cool, you guys are college buddies."

I turned my indoor grill to *high*, and pulled out

burger meat, three kinds of cheese, buns, and all the condiments.

"Yeah, but I didn't graduate."

"Oh right. I think you told me that."

"Yeah. I'd been a football player on scholarship. When I was injured, that was the end of the scholarship and I couldn't afford to keep going."

She raised her bottle toward me. "You've done well for yourself. Congrats."

I looked around my kick-ass place, and was instantly pissed at myself for not appreciating how far I'd come. But that elusive college degree was the one thing beyond my reach. It was like a pesky song playing over and over in your head that you can't get rid of.

You may have accomplished a lot, but you're still missing something...

It haunted me. And before Cal had recently come around, dragging me onto his security team, it had finally made it to the top of my to-do list.

I was going to finish, dammit. Not because I needed to for some job or other. No, it was going to be solely for my own edification. No one else's.

But it was on hold, at least for the time being.

"Thanks. I am very fortunate. I left private security with enough money to live well for the rest of my life. I have no complaints."

I sat across from Lill as we dove into our burgers, hers with bleu cheese, and mine with sharp cheddar.

My indoor grill was the bomb and had really stepped up my burger game.

"This is so good," Lill moaned, a blob of ketchup landing on her chin.

I reached over the counter with my napkin. "Here. Let me get that," I said, dabbing at her mess.

Her gaze locked with mine and she slowly set her burger down. Her deep brown eyes, captivating by any measure, were such a contrast to her vividly red hair and pale, freckled skin.

I'd never seen anyone quite like her.

"Are you finished?" I asked.

She just nodded.

I made quick work of cleaning the kitchen while she had another beer.

"I'll show you to your room and give you some clothes. If you're not too tired yet, we can watch a movie or something."

Her face perked up. "That sounds great. A diversion would be lovely. I usually write at night, but this evening, I think I'm just going to let my brain chill."

While Lill got settled in, I called Cal.

"The whole thing is strange, man. I'm still not clear on where the dude who tried to make off with her came from. These folks are aggressive. More aggressive than we'd expected they'd be."

Cal was silent for a moment. "You're right. We may have underestimated their operation. But they've also underestimated ours."

He had a point. There weren't many people out there with the skills that Cal, Thorn, and I had. As a team, we were pretty formidable, if I did say so myself.

But not infallible. And that was vital to remember.

"I have a thought, Cal. I don't know how much the von Malsens know. But I'd like to suggest we keep tonight's incident from them, at least for the time being. I don't want to trust people until I know they are one hundred percent worthy of it."

"Dex, I've worked for them for a couple years now. I feel like I know my client—"

"I'm sure you do," I interrupted, "but think of me as a fresh pair of eyes. I'm coming into this with a different perspective and I think there's no harm in doing things my way for a bit."

He released a long exhale. "All right. I trust your instincts."

A few moments later, Lill joined me in the living room wearing my hilariously oversized sweats, and settled into the sofa next to me. She chose the movie *It's Complicated* with Meryl Streep, which looked beyond horrible. But I figured I could suffer through ninety minutes of it, for her sake.

Ten minutes into the movie, she was sound asleep.

CHAPTER 19

Dex

"Whoa."
I woke up and turned over, the morning sun burning my eyes. And who lay beside me in bed, but Lill.

She stirred lightly, her red hair fanning over my sheets and across my chest.

Um, how…?

Never mind. It didn't matter.

"Lill," I whispered. "Lill?"

"Mmmm," she murmured, slowly opening one eye. "I woke up in the middle of the night on the sofa. I was afraid, so I slipped into your bed. I hope you don't mind."

Did I mind? Was she fucking crazy?

I wrapped a shock of her hair around my fingers and was amazed by its silkiness. I'd bet the rest of her was at least as pleasing.

I slid over the sheets and placed a hand on her cheek. Then, in an abrupt movement, I rolled her on top of me until I could run my hands under her baggy sweatshirt, and grind my cock against the sweats covering her pussy.

She bent down and kissed my ear.

Pulling the sweatshirt over her head, I was faced with her firm, round tits, which I pushed together to bury my face in.

"You're beautiful, Lill," I murmured as I moved between licking each of her nipples.

In another sudden movement, I flipped her onto her back, shimmying the sweatpants down over her hips. I parted her legs slowly, running my fingers through her wet excitement. When she shook with a tremor, I opened her pussy with my tongue, lapping her from front to back.

"Oh god," she moaned, writhing under me.

I poised a finger at her opening and ventured inside to my first knuckle.

Fuck, she was tight.

Then I eased my finger the rest of the way in, moving it in the *come here* motion that I hoped she'd respond to.

And she sure did.

"Oh god, Dex, I'm gonna come," she whispered hoarsely.

Her hips began to buck against my face, and when I settled in on her clit, she nearly went through the roof.

An orgasm hit her like a freight train, and it was all I could do to keep us both on the bed.

I put the finger that had been deep inside her pussy into her mouth, and she greedily sucked it clean.

That was a good sign. I liked a woman who could suck things clean.

After we'd showered and I'd fed her eggs and bacon, I gave her the quick version of my conversation with Cal the night before.

"We don't want you to go to work today."

She frowned. "Huh? I can't do that."

"You can and you will."

Her mouth dropped open, no doubt to say something smart assed, when she snapped it shut again.

She was learning. Which was good. The next incident might not end as nicely as last night's had.

"You'll call in sick today to the von Malsens. Thorn is over there and will assess the situation. This will give us a better idea of what we're up against."

"Are you kidding?" she asked.

Jesus, after what had happened the night before, was she still going to be difficult?

"You have your laptop. You can spend the day working on your writing here."

When I pointed that out, her face softened. The downside of calling in, like pissing off her boss Amalia, suddenly took a backseat to the possibilities of a free day.

Cal knew what was driving my caution. A Colombian family I'd worked with years before had suffered a tragic loss that still haunted me. My client's lovely wife was kidnapped and held for ransom, something not uncommon in Bogota at the time. The ransom was paid, but the wife wasn't brought to the pickup spot we were sent to. She was never seen again.

I'd left Colombia shortly after that and taken some time to travel and clear my head. Of course I wasn't as devastated as my client, who'd lost his wife, and his children, who'd lost their mother, but the nightmares were unrelenting.

I wasn't sure I could survive another one of those. Especially if it happened to the lovely Lill.

I couldn't deny it. She was a beautiful, sparkling woman. The kind I'd imagined meeting when I'd moved to New York. Instead, the women I typically met were either completely married to their jobs or looking for a sugar daddy to cover their bills.

When it came down to it, I hadn't come across anyone I really felt was my equal. Until now.

Lill tapped away for a few hours on her laptop

while I worked in my den. Around lunchtime, I offered her something to eat.

It was nice having her in my home, working in the next room. Something about it was comforting. And warm.

"So," I said as I put together turkey sandwiches, "Thorn called and told me that Amalia was not happy about your not coming in today. So be prepared for that."

"Guess she doesn't give a shit that I was fake-sick. Nice lady."

I just didn't get that woman. She was fortunate in so many ways, but was so sorely lacking in empathy.

It was like the universe had given her every little thing she'd ever wanted, but forgot one of the most important—how to treat other human beings. It was a shame. And a sad way to go through life.

"How long do you plan to keep working for them, the von Malsens?" I asked. I highly doubted it was a long-term gig for her.

She laughed. "Not a moment longer than I have to. In fact, I have a job interview tomorrow with a fashion magazine. I'm really excited."

"Holy shit, no kidding. That's awesome. You'll knock it out of the park. I know you will."

My instincts about things were usually right, and in this case, I really, really hoped they were.

CHAPTER 20

Lill

Just when I thought nothing could get worse than being almost abducted from a corner store when trying to pick up a bottle of cheap white wine, it did.

And then there was the small fact that I'd messed around with two of the security guards tasked with keeping me safe from said abductors.

What the fuck was wrong with me?

"You know, you should just move in here with me permanently. I have way too much space, and we would have so much fun," Beebie said, sipping her coffee.

I'd never had a friend like her. Which was all the more reason *not* to take advantage.

"Thank you, Beebs. You are so amazing. I know I need to make some decisions. I haven't even been back to my own apartment since it was broken into. I have to clean up that mess, for one thing, and then figure out whether to give my notice."

My neighbors wouldn't miss me. No one in that building ever spoke to anyone. I could lie dead in my apartment for weeks and the only way anyone would suspect was if my rotting body stunk.

That didn't mean I wanted to crash at Beebie's forever, either. Even though her place looked like a spread from *Architectural Digest*.

But first things first. I had a job interview to focus on and nothing was going to distract me from that.

Not Dex's skillful tongue exploring between my legs. Not Cal's firm grip on the back of my neck as he brought our lips together.

Nope. Wasn't going to think about any of that, at all.

"Okay. Let me see you," Beebie said, making a circle with her finger so I'd rotate.

I modeled my black Zara suit with the wide, cropped pants and matching jacket. I felt good. It was a *cool girl* outfit and it gave me a shit ton of confidence.

"Damn. Looking good," she said as I twisted my crazy hair into a messy-but-not-too-messy bun at the nape of my neck. "Here. Wear my good luck hoops," she said, pulling them out of her ears and handing them to me.

"Oh my god, Beebs," I said, choking up. "You bitch. You're going to make me cry, and it took me half an hour to put my eye makeup on."

She jumped up to hug me. "You're gonna kill it."

Not fifteen minutes later, Thorn and I pulled into the parking garage across the street from Beauté, my favorite fashion magazine of all time. I'd been reading it since I was old enough to have babysitting money, and here I was, about to walk through their doors. I took several deep breaths so I didn't fangirl all over them.

I needed to play it cool. And I was going to.

Thorn looked up at the building, scrunching his eyebrows behind his dark aviators. "What is *beauty?*" he asked, pointing at the sign.

I laughed. "It's a magazine for women. And it's pronounced *bay-you-tay.*"

"Okay. Cool. Go do your thing, and I'll wait in the lobby. Good luck."

"Thanks, Thorn."

I strolled—so that I wouldn't run, jump up and down, or scream with excitement—over to the building's front desk and told them who I was. They let me know someone would be right down to get me.

I casually leaned on the counter like I was cool as shit and glanced over at Thorn, who was going back and forth between his phone, and scanning the lobby over the top of his sunglasses. God, when these guys were on duty, they didn't get a moment of rest. But I guess all the looking around for trouble eventually became second nature.

And if that were the case, how the hell did they ever shut it off?

"You must be Lillian. Come on in," a model-like woman about my age said. "I'm Jade."

Why did fashion girls get all the cool as shit names? You never, ever met one named Sue.

The front desk guy opened the security gate for me, and I extended my hand. "Feel free to call me Lill."

"Okay, Lill," she said with a big smile. "Hey, is that guy over there with you?" she asked, gesturing with her chin.

Thorn was looking right at us.

Shit.

But I shook my head anyway. "No. He's not."

After the elevator had taken us up to the twentieth—or thirtieth?—floor, Jade walked me through a field of pretty girls and handsome gay guys at their desks, all focused, I supposed, on the next issue of the magazine.

We arrived in a conference room with walls covered in framed Beauté covers from years past. A thrill ran through me when I realized I remembered most of them.

"Love this," I said, gesturing at the walls.

Jade nodded with a smile. "Isn't it cool?"

I took a seat opposite her. "Thanks for inviting me today. I'm such a fan of the magazine."

"You're welcome. So, Lill, I love all your writing experience. What are you doing right now?"

"I've finished one romance novel and am looking for an agent, and I'm working on my second."

I sure as hell wasn't going to tell her I was also the von Malsens' cleaning lady who, by the way, was also being chased by bad guys.

"Cool," she said. "So, this internship goes for six months—"

Wait. What? Did she just say *internship*?

No, no, no. Please no.

"Jade, I thought this was for a permanent position."

Her eyes widened. "Oh. I'm sorry. It's not."

Oh god.

All my excitement leading up to this day, and the excitement at actually being under the roof of Beauté, collapsed, crumpling into a little ball, like a piece of paper being tossed into a trash can.

Keep it together girl.

Jade pressed her lips together kindly. I wanted to hate her, but I just couldn't bring myself to. "I take it you're not interested in an internship?"

"Well, I've done a couple internships, so I was kind of thinking I'd checked that box," I said with a casual laugh.

Don't cry. Do. Not. Cry.

She smiled in return. "I'm so sorry. When the HR

person called you to come in, she should have made it clear what this was for."

Had she? And in my excitement, I just didn't listen?

"Well, Jade, if an internship is all you have, then let's talk about that," I said cheerfully.

She filled me in on the ins and outs of interning at Beauté, which were not so different from internships anywhere else. While she extolled the benefits of having Beauté on my resume, I had a second to slow the racing thoughts in my head.

Could I accept an internship?

How the hell would I pay my bills?

"It's unpaid, I take it?" I asked.

"It is unpaid. Sorry."

Fuck, fuck, fuckity, fuck.

But I didn't want to close the door altogether. Who knew if I'd ever have the chance to walk through the doors of Beauté again?

Jade walked me to the elevator.

"I'm definitely interested, despite the misunderstanding. I'd love to work with you, Jade."

"Thanks so much Lill. It was a pleasure meeting you. We'll be in touch."

When I reached the lobby, it was a miracle I didn't dissolve into a puddle of nothingness, devastated as I was.

Thorn jumped up when he saw me. "How'd it go?"

I didn't want to talk about it. I was afraid I'd start to cry.

"Fine," I mumbled.

Even though he had his sunglasses on, I could tell he was looking at me like I was full of shit. But that was okay, because I was.

When we arrived at the von Malsens', I rushed into the restroom to change and hide evidence of my interview. Not that anyone would be surprised I was trying to better my lot, it was just that I didn't need them in my business before I had something definitive.

"Hi, Amalia. Sorry I missed yesterday. I'm feeling much better now," I said when I found her on the terrace.

She lowered her sunglasses and glared at me. "Good. Because there's a lot to do."

Really?

I got to work and ran into Thorn when I was Swiffering the von Malsens' bedroom hardwood floor.

"Hey, Lill," he said quietly, looking around, "the reason she's so pissed is that Robbie had a temper tantrum when he found out you weren't coming in, and basically told Amalia he likes you better than her or the nanny."

I stifled a laugh. No wonder she'd been extra rude to me. But I'd be kind of upset if my kid liked the cleaning lady better than me, too.

"Thanks for telling me."

Before I left that night to head out to my writing class, I asked Amalia about my book again.

"Have you had the chance to read my romance?" I asked her with a big smile.

"No."

Well, then.

She looked up from whatever it was she was reading. "I haven't gotten to it. Relax. Rome wasn't built in a day."

CHAPTER 21

Lill

"Did you and your decorator friend enjoy the party last week?" Bert asked as I settled into my seat in our writing group.

"Sure."

Actually, it had been nice until a particular asshole decided to insult me for being a cleaning lady.

He leaned closer. "You know, I get invited to things like that all the time. I could bring you."

Shit. Of course I wanted to go to more parties like that. I just didn't want Bert to be the gatekeeper to them. But until I could finagle my own invites, it looked like I'd have to put up with him.

The big question was, what would he expect in

return? Bert wasn't the kind of guy who did something out of the kindness of his heart. He lived for the *quid pro quo*.

"After class, let me get your number. That way I can invite you."

Shit. I was trapped.

As if I hadn't already had a stressful day, it was my night to read a couple pages from my latest book. As per the class rules, I'd emailed my pages the week before, and after I read them aloud, I'd get feedback from everyone.

"I don't get why you write romance, Lill," one of my classmates said.

Here we go again.

Our instructor intervened before a debate could break out. "The reason we're here is to offer feedback on each others' writing, not to ask them why they write in the genre they do."

"Thanks, Val," I said. "But I will just say to the group, as I have before, that romance stories are uplifting. They end happily, with the bad guy getting his due. Sometimes people might be in the mood for an end of the world story, but sometimes they need something positive. That's what I do. Sorry you don't like it." I threw a serious stink eye in the direction of my critic.

"It's just that I think Lill could write something with more—"

"Your pages were very good, Lill. Okay, now who's up next?" Val asked, looking around the room.

Bam. I was back. Now if only I could figure out how to swing an internship at Beauté, and not starve in the process.

After class, I broke down and gave Bert my phone number. I'd been resisting doing just that for ages, having asked that he email me if he wanted to get in touch. Something about his being able to text or call me seemed a little close. Like it would be too easy for him to really infringe on my privacy and insert himself into my life.

But after the day's non-interview interview for a magazine internship, I was going to have to swallow my distaste for Bert, and least for the short term.

"Going to the subway?" he offered as we left the building.

I looked around for Thorn, who was supposed to pick me up. "Um, no. I have a ride coming."

As if he had heard me, Thorn pulled around the corner and screeched to a stop at the curb right in front of Bert and me.

"Who's that?" Bert asked.

"Just my ride. Talk to you later."

I jumped into the front seat, grateful to be going home after a whacked day, and strangely comforted to see Thorn's strong arms and quirky smile.

CHAPTER 22

Thorn

"I can't say much, but the PI tells me he's making good progress on figuring out what the hell is going on with the von Malsens. The immediate question is, though, how do we keep Lill safe?" Cal said.

I had a feeling we'd get to the point that having us three guys escort Lill everywhere she went was no longer enough. If whoever was after her wanted her badly enough, they'd eventually find a way to get to her.

Criminals can be very highly motivated people.

I know, because I used to be one.

Unfortunately, my older brother Frankie still was. It broke my fucking heart.

In fact, he'd called me just earlier in the week.

"Yo. Thorn. We've got a job for you."

He was never going to give up.

"Frankie, I told you I was done. I'm clean now, and living a new life. Why do you keep trying to pull me back in?"

He laughed. "You, clean. Yeah right. You crack me up, little brother."

I wanted to reach through the phone and shake him. "Why is it so goddamn hard for you to understand that someone might want to go straight? Leave all the street bullshit behind?"

I could picture him pacing, like he always did when he was frustrated. "Thorn. First of all, no one quits the streets. The streets might quit you. And that's when you get carried out in a wooden box. But you don't get to walk away."

He was wrong. I already had walked away. It was the fact that I had that was so unfathomable to him.

"Second, you have our business in your blood. You can't do anything else *but* hustle."

What a fucker. Not only did I have other options, but so did he. Only he'd never realize it. Drug trafficking and all the bullshit that came along with it was so ingrained in him, there was just no going back. He'd never give it up.

And he'd never give up trying to drag me back in.

"You know, Thorn, you think you're better than all

of us now, don't you, since you turned your back on us."

My blood started to boil. It hadn't been easy going straight, and had been even tougher staying straight. That's why so many criminals fell right back into their old ways. What I'd done was fucking hard. And I was proud of it. Frankie, or anybody else, would never take that away from me.

"That's bullshit, Frankie. You could go straight too if you wanted to. I'll help you."

He burst out laughing. "That's a good one, little bro. Save your breath. Look, we need you to do a pickup for us. We're moving a lot of goods right now and need to stay on schedule."

Jesus. He didn't understand what *no* meant.

"Frankie, the answer is no—"

But he cut me off, his tone changing to something more gritty. I knew where he was going with things. I'd grown up with the fucker. "If you can't get off your ass and give us a hand, I might just have to make sure some of the guys you pissed off find out you're living in a dump over a bowling alley downtown. I'm sure they'd like to stop by and say hello. They've been asking about ya."

Jesus Christ. Would he really give away my whereabouts? Was he that desperate to drag me back into his miserable life?

"Frankie," I said quietly, "you just went too far. If I see you, or any of your goons, anywhere in my neighborhood, I'll knock your fucking teeth straight down your throat. And don't tempt me, Frankie. You know I can do it. You've seen me."

He was silent for a moment. "So that's how it is? Okay. I hear ya, bud. I'll tell you though, I'm disappointed. I taught you everything you know about the streets, and now you turn your back on me."

If I'd turned my back on him, he'd be in prison. But if he kept threatening me, I could make a few calls that would send him there in the express bus.

"Goodbye, Frankie," I said, and hung up the call.

When I'd met Cal and Dex later at Regulator, my first stop was at the bar.

"Hey, handsome," Jen said. "What can I get you?"

"How 'bout a new life?" I joked.

She flipped her long black hair back and leaned forward on the bar. "If I sold those, I'd be a rich lady. Tell me, you got some shit going on, Thorn?"

That was a good question. But was my shit any worse than anyone else's shit? I mean, for Christ's sake, I was lucky to be off the streets. Actually, I was fucking lucky to even be alive, given some of the things I'd done.

"It's all good, baby. Thanks for asking. Hey, I haven't seen your pretty wife around here lately." I pushed a twenty across the bar to cover two beers for the guys and a whiskey for me.

Her eyes brightened. "She is mega-busy. Cal hooked

her up with a job doing security in the same building where you guys are working. She started last week."

I threw an extra ten on the bar. I couldn't help it. I was a sucker for a beautiful woman, no matter what team she played on.

"Well, I'll look forward to seeing her, then. You take good care, Jen."

When I returned to the table, Cal was clinking his empty glass on the table.

"Jesus, a man could die of thirst around here," he laughed.

"Well, boo fucking hoo. I was chatting up your gorgeous business partner."

He nodded. "Gorgeous she is. But she's married to a woman."

I raised my hands as if in surrender. "I didn't say I was making the moves. I was just enjoying the scenery. Very respectfully."

The guys laughed.

"But I will say I might have some designs on our girl, Lill."

Dex and Cal looked at each other.

What? Did they know something I didn't?

"One of you guys already dating her or something?" I asked, looking from one to the other.

Assholes. At least they could have told me.

"Well, it's not that…" Cal said slowly.

Dex leaned over the table toward me, lowering his

voice. "We've both had a… taste of the lovely lady. Now, it's your turn."

Fuck yeah.

"Cal and I like to share a woman. Have you ever done that?" he added.

Jesus. If those guys knew half the shit I'd done their heads would explode.

"More or less. Care to explain further?" I said.

"It's fine if we all three want to date her. Well, at least it's fine with Cal and me," he said, looking at Cal, who nodded in agreement. "If it works for you, so much the better."

I shook my head, smiling. "Sounds kinky as fuck. I'm in."

"Now, we just have to assess whether Lill is in. She might not be. There aren't a lot of women out there who can… understand this sort of arrangement."

Cal was right. I'd seen a few women thrive on what I'll call *group activities*. Most run in the opposite direction.

Time would tell.

"So in the meantime, Cal, what are we gonna do with Lill?" Dex asked. "Personally, I think we need to take her out of town until things cool off."

Cal nodded. "I was thinking the same. We could go to my cabin up north. But the problem is, I seriously doubt she'd agree to go. And I'm not too keen on forcing her. She's strong-minded. Doesn't let anyone push her around."

"Except for that Amalia," I said.

"Isn't that the truth? I have a feeling she's saving up a few choice words for that woman, and when the time comes, she'll let them fly. It ain't gonna be pretty," Dex added.

I burst out laughing at that. I couldn't wait to see Lill put Amalia in her place. That would be an epic show.

"She could also stay at either Dex's or my place. They're both pretty much set up like fortresses. But I doubt she'd agree to that, either."

I cleared my throat. "Speaking of which, I think I'm going to have to say goodbye to my lovely little place above the bowling alley."

Cal chuckled. "I'm not so sure that's a bad thing, Thorn."

No shit.

"Got a call from my brother today."

Cal's eyes widened. "Oh shit."

"Yeah. Exactly. When I turned down his latest job, he threatened to share my whereabouts with some guys I'd rather not know where I live."

Crime. The gift that kept on giving.

"That sucks, man," Dex said. "You know, I have extra room if you want to crash at my place for a while."

Cal nodded. "I do too. I mean, I don't have the palace that Dex does, but you're welcome to take over my extra room."

Jesus. Just when you think you've hit rock bottom, the universe throws you a nice, juicy bone.

Definitely one I did nothing to deserve.

"You guys fucking rock. Seriously."

"Happy to help," Dex said, holding his beer up for a toast.

"Thank you. Thanks to both of you," I said, feeling a lump start to build in my throat.

Dammit. I hated that.

"So now I guess I'll let you fuckers fight over who gets me. But I want to warn you in advance, if I get with the lovely Miss Lill, you'll have to hear me pounding on her all fucking night long."

"Cheers to that," Cal said, laughing.

CHAPTER 23

Lill

I was never a sadder cleaning lady who lived in a studio apartment, writing stories no one would probably ever read, as when I was in Beebie's apartment.

Of course, she'd never want me to feel that way. She was a true blue friend, generous to a fault, and the biggest supporter I'd ever had.

So, *I* was the one who wondered—no, doubted—whether I'd ever see even a fraction of the success she had.

She'd worked hard, no question about it, and I was thrilled for all her success. Proud of her, even. And I loved how we'd bonded over the pervy crotch-looker guy in yoga. But would I ever have a place like hers with stark white walls and neon oversized paintings? Bright pink sofas and turquoise and yellow chairs with rugs that looked like they were designed by someone on acid?

If you took each component of her home, aside from the white walls, you might feel simultaneously nauseous and manic. But the true effect, when everything was in its place and she'd waved her magic wand over an insane collection of color and textures, was mesmerizing. Some how, some way, it worked.

She had style. It was what she was known for, and what she was rapidly becoming famous for.

It was fucking awesome, and couldn't have happened to a more deserving person.

But were digs like this in the cards for me? I somehow doubted it, and as much as Beebie insisted I live with her, no such arrangement would ever be permanent. I had to figure out my own shit. If not now, then pretty soon.

So while I was sponging off her I figured the least I could do was clean house, especially since I had gotten to be such a pro at it, thanks to YouTube and the fantastic opportunity the von Malsen family had afforded me.

I also needed to get back to my own apartment, straighten out the mess it was in, and decide where I would live next. I knew the guys wouldn't let me move back there, especially not with all the security issues the building had. Hell, they'd even made me promise I wouldn't go near the place without at least one of them accompanying me, that's how convinced they were the place was a disaster waiting to happen, and that spending any more time there than absolutely necessary would be the end of me.

It seemed like a lot of things could be the end of me, lately. Like messing around with the guys who were guarding my life.

In what world was that normal?

The three of them were hot as hell and it was all I could do to think straight when they were around. Thorn was the only one I hadn't kissed yet. In fact, he was the only one I hadn't done anything with. But he was also the one I was most likely to mess around with. He and his rough-around-the-edges swagger were the stuff women dreamed of, took off their panties for, and forgot their names over.

I was in deep trouble. As much as I knew I had to stay away from those guys, if I was honest with myself, it just wasn't going to happen.

Beebie had been bugging me to try online dating. Or try it again, I should say. After a few creepy liars—one was engaged to be married in a couple months, and the other said he was founder of a tech company but actually lived in his parents' basement and worked for Door Dash—I'd thrown in the towel. I'd meet guys the natural, old-school way, by being *out and about*. Online dating was too contrived and pressure filled. You had an unnaturally short amount of time to impress someone who, in any other circumstance, like meeting through friends, you could get to know over time through several low-pressure gatherings. Online dating worked fine for some people. Me, not so much.

And then there were the dick pics. One of my girlfriends had started a Facebook group for dick pics. Word got out about it, and so many girls in New York were posting there that the group got shut down for pornography or some such. It was fun while it lasted.

And even if I did want to give online dating a shot again, how the hell would I manage that with hulking bodyguards following me everywhere I went?

Hello, New Date. I'm Lill. And this is my security detail. Look at me wrong, and you may end up dead.

Not the kind of outing likely to result in a second date.

Plus, Cal, Dex, and Thorn would probably think I was a big ho-bag anyway. Why was I collecting dudes online when I had real Grade-A beef right there in front of me?

on my way. be there in five

Shit. I'd lost track of time and now Cal was on his way to take me to work.

One positive thing about the shit show that had become my endangered life? It was freaking awesome to be driven to and from work every day. No bus or subway for me, no sir. I was sired around just like all the rich ladies.

It almost made up for having to pick up Amalia's dirty undies.

I scrambled to the elevator, pressing the button ten times like I always did when I was in a hurry. When I reached the lobby, Cal was waiting out front, hands on the steering wheel, his head turned in my direction like he'd known the actual second I'd come out of the building's front door.

For a moment, I wished I'd put something nicer on than the faded Bad Company T-shirt I'd gotten at Goodwill. But it didn't make sense to wear anything nicer if you were going to get it dirty, did it?

On the other hand, I had to admit, I'd put on a little lip gloss and mascara. In fact, I'd been doing that the last few days. Not for the guys or anything, but for me.

Yeah, right.

"Hi, Cal," I said, pulling my door closed.

"Morning, gorgeous," he said, his gaze locked on mine.

Oh my. Was this how my day was going to go? How would I ever get anything done?

We sat looking at each other and dammit, my pulse was starting to race.

I had to break the spell. "So, are you gonna drive? Or should I take the subway?"

He laughed and put the car in gear. "Lill, if you keep behaving like that, I'll make you walk and follow you in the car to keep an eye on you."

Holy shit. Was that a little growl I heard in his voice?

And was that a growing warmth I felt between my legs?

Good god. I was fucked.

So to hide what I was knew was my furiously blushing face, I pulled out my phone as if I had something important to do.

And, there was an email from Beauté.

Dear Lill,

Thanks so much for coming by last week. It was great meeting you.

We wanted to let you know we found an intern who was better suited to our immediate needs. But please be sure to keep in touch...

Oh my god. I couldn't even get an *unpaid* job. Never mind a fucking paid one.

Did I have the black cloud from hell hanging over my head or what? Seriously, universe. Wasn't it enough that someone was trying to kidnap and possibly kill me? And now the best I can do career-wise is clean some rich lady's house?

My throat tightened and my eyes burned. I knew what was coming, and it wasn't going to be pretty. Turning my face toward the passenger window, I tried to hide my tears from Cal, but my sniffles gave me away.

To his credit, he only glanced my way once or twice, remaining focused on traffic.

I blew my nose. "Sorry. I just got some not so great news."

He reached over and took my hand. "I'm sorry. You want to talk about it?"

I shrugged. "I'd met with the folks at Beauté for what I thought was a job interview. It turned out to be just for an internship, which I wasn't selected for anyway."

He squeezed my hand, and I had to say it felt nice.

"That sucks. But that also means there's something better for you out there. Everyone gets a shit sandwich at some point. You are getting yours right now."

I had to laugh at that. "Shit sandwich?"

He nodded. "It's the perfect term for when life is fucking you over."

"Well, what was one of your shit sandwiches?" I asked.

He sucked in his breath and hesitated.

Maybe I shouldn't have asked.

"When I was on the force, my partner got shot on a routine call."

Oh my god. That was serious stuff.

"I'm so sorry."

He steered the car into the von Malsen's parking

garage. "Thank you. I still have nightmares about it. He left behind a wife and twin kids."

Fuck. Talk about perspective. If I made it out of this thing with the bad guys after me, I'd really have nothing to complain about. Sure, things were sucky right now, but I had my whole life ahead of me.

"Thanks for sharing that, Cal. I appreciate it," I said in the elevator on the way up. I extended my hand and gave his a squeeze just like he'd done mine. It was the least I could do.

We walked all the way down the hallway holding hands and just before we got to the von Malsen's door, Cal gave me a kiss on the cheek.

"Well. Here we go. Another day at the office," he said.

Cal disappeared to wherever he went when he was at the von Malsens' and I got to work cleaning all the crap off Amalia's floor. The second she went out somewhere with Robbie, I dialed Beebie.

"Hey, Beebs."

"Oh shit. What's wrong?"

Dammit. Her caring voice brought the tears back. I told her my latest woe while using toilet paper from Amalia's bathroom to blow my nose.

"Shit, Beebs. I just feel like the biggest loser."

She sighed. "You. Are. Not. A loser. Look, when you get off work, we'll meet for drinks."

"Oh, that sounds amazing, but I'm supposed to go to

a thing with that guy Bert. He promised to introduce me to some people."

"Well then go, and when you get home, we'll have a glass of wine and celebrate."

"Celebrate what?" I asked.

"Nothing and everything. Do we need to have a reason?"

Holy shit. I loved that girl.

CHAPTER 24

Lill

"Hey, Bert," I said with forced enthusiasm. Which meant no enthusiasm at all.

"Lill. Glad you survived that dressing down in writing class the other day," he said.

Huh?

"What are you talking about?"

He frowned. "You know, that woman who was dumping on romance books. Although, I guess you're used to that stuff by now."

"Used to what?" I asked, although I knew the answer. I just wanted to make him say it.

He rolled his eyes. "Well, being the Walmart of the literary world."

What. The. Fuck.

He was lucky we were in public because I wanted to stab him with the first sharp thing I could get my hands on.

"Bert, that's a really shitty thing to say. Do you ever think before you open your mouth?"

I stormed away, pushing through the smiling crowd, desperate for the ladies' room. There, I could regroup and decide if I was going to stick around for the night, or feed Bert arsenic and pretend that I hadn't murdered him.

I locked myself into one of the stalls and sat on top of the toilet seat with my head in my hands.

I shouldn't even be at this party without one of the guys from the security team. I was taking a risk. A big risk. Someone could grab me at any time, like they had in that convenience store. If I hadn't dropped that bottle of wine and caught Dex's attention, god only knew where I'd be today.

But the truth was, I didn't want the guys to see me with Bert. It would have been too embarrassing. The guy was such a creep, and as if there weren't already enough evidence of his douchey-ness, he had to pile on the insults on the one night I agreed to go out with him. So, again, I'd sneaked out of the house.

Fuck my life.

I left the bathroom stall and touched up my lip gloss. I was going to find Bert and tell him to shove his stupid comments up his ass.

But as I got closer to him, I saw he was chatting with someone I was pretty sure was a literary agent. Wow. He really did know people.

I stood right behind him to eavesdrop where I wouldn't be noticed, and scrolled through my phone like I was looking for something.

"Look, like I said, her work's not that good, but I'd really appreciate your talking to her," he said.

Holy crap. Was he talking about me? I looked around.

Of course he was. Who else would he be talking about?

The guy sipped his drink and nodded. "Sure man. I'll help you out. It's the least I could do for the guy who gets me the best shit in New York. And what's the harm if she's as hot as you say?" He snickered.

What the fuck? Bert was a dealer? And now he was my pimp?

"Thanks, man. And if I get to fuck her, your next gram is on me," he said, clinking glasses with the guy.

"Absolutely, my friend."

Oh god.

Head down, I bolted straight for the door, hoping I wouldn't vomit right there in the party.

Just when I thought shit couldn't get any shittier...

"Beebs?" I said into my cell as soon as she'd answered and I was safely ensconced in a cab whose driver didn't look murderous. "Make sure the wine is ready. I'm heading home."

CHAPTER 25

Cal

"Where are we going?"

Lill's question was followed by a big sigh.

God, she could be a pain in the ass. Most people stuck on the island of Manhattan would be thrilled to have a day outside the city.

"A small town about two hours north. My family has an old cabin on a few acres."

Unimpressed, she continued scrolling through her phone in the backseat of Dex's SUV, where she sat next to Thorn.

He looked up from his book. "Sounds awesome. Relax, Lill. You may just enjoy yourself."

I caught her rolling her eyes when I glanced back at her.

It hadn't been easy to find a day when we were all free and the von Malsens' security needs were being covered by the weekend team. But as soon as I had, I'd decided an outing would be the perfect thing for some of the stress we were all under.

I'd apparently underestimated Lill's reluctance to leave the city, even for just one day, and now she was giving us guys major attitude.

Which kind of turned me on.

I kept having visions of bending her over my knee to teach her a little lesson…

Down boy.

We pulled off the main road onto the dirt one leading to the cabin, and I popped the truck into four-wheel drive.

"Yeah," Thorn yelled, bracing himself, "that's what I'm talking about."

He rolled his window down and hung out, slapping the leaves and branches whipping the sides of the car.

Lill, on the other hand, had a death grip on the 'oh shit' handle, and squeezed her eyes shut through every pothole we bounced over.

We were going only ten or fifteen miles an hour, but I didn't want to scare the shit out of her, so I slowed down further.

Dex turned around from the passenger seat. "Lill, are you gonna be okay?"

We rolled through another rut in the road, and she bounced off her seat, nearly bumping her head.

"Yeah. This is awesome. I was really in the mood for four wheeling today. Hey Cal, you said you had a cabin in the woods, but you didn't say we had to drive through hell to get to it," she called to the front seat.

Jesus. Was she going to be disagreeable all day?

I was thinking of something smart-assed to say when Thorn beat me to it. "Baby, if you think this is hell, you've had a pretty nice goddamn life."

Leave it to Thorn to lay it out.

He was right. And his logic broke through her shit mood.

She laughed. She actually laughed. "Well, it is pretty," she said, looking out the window at the lush foliage.

"And... here we are," I said, pulling up in front of the cabin.

Damn, it had been a long time since anyone had been there. I hoped the house hadn't been taken over by rodents.

But the place, rustic as it was, was tightly sealed from the outside world like a time capsule, still stuffed with the hand-me-down furniture my parents had filled the place up with so long ago. Even my mom's red-checkered tablecloth was on the kitchen table.

"Holy fuck, I love this place," Thorn bellowed, doing a lap around the exterior of the house, partly having a good time but also partly making a security check.

"Did you come here as a kid, Cal?" I asked.

I looked around the cabin. "I sure did. Sometimes stayed up here all summer. I don't know how my mom stood it. Half the time there was no hot water and every time it stormed, we lost electricity."

But that was what had made it so idyllic.

"What do you think, Lill?" I asked, holding my breath.

If she couldn't deal with a little rustic, she was not the girl for me. And I suspected Dex and Thorn felt the same way.

"It's... charming," she said, looking around the living room.

Well, it was a step in the right direction.

"Okay guys, who's on patrol first?" I asked.

"Patrol? What do you mean, patrol?" Lill asked.

I looked at the other guys. We'd not briefed Lill because we didn't want her to worry.

"I'm up first," Dex said, checking his hip for his weapon. "We're taking turns walking the property, Lill. It's part of the job."

Her eyes widened. "Did you just check for a *gun* or something?" she asked in a wobbly voice, pointing at Dex's side.

"Yes. We're always armed."

She pressed her lips together and grew a little paler.

I sometimes forgot how unfamiliar civilians were with the way our world worked.

"C'mon, Lill. Let's take a walk around the property with Thorn. Dex has work to do," I said.

I was dying to take her hand but didn't want to push it.

"So your family owns all this property?" she asked when we'd walked in silence for a few minutes.

"They did. Now it's mine."

Fuck, I'd forgotten how sweet the air smelled, I'd been in Manhattan for so long.

We came across a path I used to take all the time when I was a kid. It was now so overgrown that if I hadn't known it was there, I'd never have noticed it.

I turned to Lill and Thorn. "You guys feel like doing a little bushwhacking?"

Thorn grinned. Of course. "Hell, yeah."

We both looked at Lill.

She looked down at her sneaker-covered feet and pulled her baseball cap on tighter. "Okay. Sure. Let's do it."

"That's the fucking spirit, girl," Thorn said, patting her on the back.

CHAPTER 26

Cal

Thorn and I led the way through a tunnel of bushes, branches, and spider webs to clear the way as much as possible for Lill. But she hung with us, stepping over obstacles and holding back the foliage that would otherwise smack her in the face.

After ten minutes of this, I was waiting for Lill to pull the plug and demand that we head back. And I think she might have been about to, when we emerged into a clearing.

"Holy shit. Look at this," Thorn yelled, running like a little kid toward the pond my grandfather had built decades ago.

I looked at Lill, whose eyes widened. "It's beautiful.

Oh my gosh. Who would have thought this was back here?"

We walked toward the water's edge and even though it was overgrown with weeds and other growth, the beauty was no less evident than it had been years ago.

"Check this out," I said, pointing to a wooden bench.

Lill traced her fingers along a carving of my name, which I'd made when I was about twelve or so.

"My mother was so mad I carved up this bench. She'd hounded and hounded my dad to put it in and when he finally did, I defaced it."

I had to laugh. Mom really had been pissed about that.

Lill took a seat facing the water. "But look how precious it is all these years later, making you laugh."

She was right.

"Oh my. Is Thorn doing what I think he's doing?" she asked, pointing to him on the rickety little dock where my dad used to tie his two-person rowboat.

Holy shit. Thorn had stripped all his clothes off and waded into the water.

No freaking way.

"Thorn, you are crazy," I called.

He waved us in. "You're right about that. Now c'mon you two. The water's awesome."

I couldn't remember the last time I'd skinny dipped in the pond.

Oh, what the hell. I stood and began stripping too.

"Woo, this is great," Thorn yelled, backstroking to the middle of the water.

"Are you coming, Lill?" I asked, looking at her sitting on the bench with her mouth wide open.

"Um, well, uh… oh, why not. I made it all the way here."

I stepped into the pond, the soft bottom squishing between my toes. I ducked under to get completely wet and when I came back up was transported to my childhood by the taste and smell of the water.

"Holy shit. This is great!" I said, splashing Thorn.

"Hey, smart ass," he said, giving up his backstroke to splash me back.

I noticed Thorn looking over my shoulder while he tried to move waves of water with his huge arms, and I turned.

Our girl Lill was gingerly stepping into the pond. Naked.

And fucking A if she wasn't more beautiful than I ever thought she'd be.

Her pale, freckled skin reflected the bright sun as she held her arms out for balance. Her lovely tits jiggled the smallest amount as she walked, and her waist and hips curved in the way men dream of.

Stop staring.

"Ooooh look at the naked Lill," Thorn hollered, splashing water in her direction.

I could always count on Thorn to ease any

awkwardness with his stream of consciousness comments.

Lill laughed and jumped in the rest of the way. "Oh my god. This is chilly," she said, wrapping her arms around herself.

"Move around a little. You'll warm up," Thorn said, returning to his backstroke.

Suddenly, Lill screamed.

Thorn and I went on instant defense. But we were naked. There wasn't much we could do.

"Ew, I stepped on something gross," she said, paddling toward me. "Ew, ew, ew."

When she reached me, she held out her hand.

I pulled her to me. Why not?

Holding her under the arms, I twirled her in the water, first one way, and then the other.

She dropped her head back and squealed, having forgotten her freak out of a moment earlier.

Then, I lay her back with one hand underneath to keep her afloat, marveling at the long red hair fanning out from her head. From the other side of the pond, Thorn watched.

I ran my free hand down the front of her wet body, pausing to make circles around her breasts, then her belly button, and last, the narrow strip of pubic hair just above her slit. She squirmed under me a little, closing her eyes and smiling at the sensation of the warm sun and my touch.

I dragged a finger between the lips of her pussy and

was pleased to find her slick with excitement. I placed my finger in my mouth for a taste, and knew I had to have more.

"What do we have here, kids?" Thorn asked, moving closer while stroking his hard cock.

There was no hiding mine, either, as it bobbed in the water, bouncing against Lill's arm.

Thorn placed a hand under Lill's head, and brought his mouth to hers, his wet face dripping onto hers. But she raised her arms and pulled him to her with the kind of hunger I thought she might possess, and kissed him hard.

"Hold her up, Thorn," I said as I moved to her feet.

He placed a hand under her back as I floated her legs apart.

Her pussy was beautiful and pink, partially above and partially below the water's surface. So I hoisted her under the knees onto my arms, pulling her out of the water just enough to put my mouth on her.

As soon as I did, she took one hand off Thorn's head, and placed it on mine, pushing me into her, demanding more.

Our girl was greedy.

And I loved it.

Holding her up, I pressed a finger against her opening and as it slid in, went to work on her with my tongue. She began to tremble, and Thorn, who kept holding her afloat, bent to kiss and lick her tits.

She moaned, pushing against my arms and into my face.

"Oh my god," she whispered. "I'm coming… I'm coming…"

Well, fuck.

I kept pumping her with two fingers until she begged me to stop.

"Hey. Can we get out of the pond?" she asked, laughing.

"Oh hell yeah," Thorn said, picking her up and taking her to the water's edge until she had solid ground to stand on.

We followed her to a soft, grassy patch in the shade of an oak tree.

"I want someone to fuck me. Now," she demanded.

Well, who was I to say no?

I ran to my jeans and came back with a condom that I threw in Thorn's direction. His face lit up, and he sheathed himself.

"Here, baby," I said, pulling Lill down to her knees facing me.

I lay back on my elbows, directing her mouth to my cock, and Thorn got behind her. As soon as she'd engulfed my hard on, Thorn drove inside her all the way, riding her until his legs smacked loudly against her ass.

She took me to the back of her throat and gagged at first, but then relaxed, pistoning on my dick until I was ready to explode.

With Thorn pumping behind her, she started to tremble again, and I knew her orgasm was close. It was a good thing, because there was no fucking way I could hold my own.

"Are you ready, baby?" I bellowed, thrusting into her mouth one last time. I shook as I emptied my load, and when I pulled out, some of it dribbled down her chin in one of the hottest fucking things I'd ever seen.

Thorn was close behind. "Oh yeah," he roared, driving faster as Lill screamed with her own orgasm.

"Oh god, oh god," she moaned, her head bucking up and down. "Yes, Thorn. Fuck me like that."

When they'd finished, I lay her down on the grass and we wrapped our arms around her from both sides.

I wouldn't have minded staying like that for a long, long time.

I glanced around the pond out of force of habit and saw Dex on the other side of it, smiling and saluting us.

I lay back and just started to laugh.

CHAPTER 27

Lill

My day in the country turned out a little different than I thought it would. I'd pictured hanging out on a porch swing, sipping lemonade or maybe something harder, while I watched the guys play catch or maybe even tackle on the front lawn. Of course, when they were done, they'd quench their thirst with some cool brews.

Instead of the charming, genteel setting I'd imagined, things turned into a down and dirty sex fest.

I was not complaining. But I did feel a little awkward, just as I had the first time Cal had kissed me in Beebie's building and Dex had gone down on me in his apartment. I mean, it was all hot as shit, but I worked with these guys.

And they were kinky as hell.

So, with Dex driving me across town, I pretty much just sat with my hands folded in my lap, looking out the front or passenger side window so I could avoid even glancing his way. I was on my way to an important meeting and I didn't need my pulse going into overdrive looking at the way his hot as shit button-down shirt stretched over his huge biceps, or how his flawless skin glowed in the sun light.

Down girl.

He was driving me to a meeting with an agent. Incredibly, it was the agent who Bert had trashed talked me to. Of course, the one Amalia had mentioned never materialized. No big surprise there. But Bert's guy called me and when I demurred, saying I wasn't ready for an agent meeting, he'd insisted, saying his agency was looking to get into the romance market, and at the very least, wouldn't it be great to establish contact for future work?

He'd also hinted around that I might introduce him to other romance authors. I fibbed and told him I'd be glad to, but the truth was the people I knew were pretty established, and not only did they already have representation, even if they didn't, they wouldn't go with someone new to romance like he was.

So maybe he wasn't the douche-y coke head I'd

thought he was the night I overheard Bert and him talking.

Actually, I was still pretty sure he was a douche-y coke head, but who knew what might come of a meeting, and whether I could learn a few nuggets about how publishing worked, anyway.

So much for principles.

"I think this is the place," I said, checking the address on my phone with the one on the building where we'd stopped.

"Cool. Text me when you're done and I'll swing by to get you. And don't forget, okay? Text me from inside the building and wait there until I arrive." He pressed his gorgeous lips together as if to underscore how serious he was.

I nodded. "I promise, Dex. It probably won't be long. Definitely under a half hour."

God, he was sweet.

Before I jumped out of the SUV, I pulled the visor mirror down for one last check of my makeup, threw a casual smile Dex's way, and headed in.

A meeting with an agent was at least as important as a job interview, at least to me, but for some reason, I wasn't nervous.

Low expectations, I supposed.

"So you're Lill. I'm Hugh. Nice to meet you," he said, jumping up from his desk and extending his hand.

"Can I get you some water?" he asked, using the universal hand gesture of drinking something.

I took a seat opposite his massive desk, and looked over his shoulder at the sprawling view of Manhattan. Literary agents must make a good living.

No wonder he could afford cocaine.

"Sure, water would be great. Thanks, Hugh."

He reached behind his desk and produced two room-temperature Perriers, one for himself and the other for me.

He must save the cold ones for the high rollers.

Leaning back in his chair, he twisted his cap off and threw it in the direction of his trash can.

He missed.

"Now how do you know Bert?" he asked, leaning onto his desk with his elbows.

"We're in a class together. A writing class. I've known him for a while. And how do you know him, Hugh?" I asked, even though I was pretty sure I already knew.

He hesitated, which told me all I needed to know. But of course he spun a lie, because guys like him always did.

"Oh, um, I know him from around. You know."

Yup. He was a coke head and Bert was definitely a coke dealer.

God, what an asshole Bert was. He'd always pretended to be independently wealthy, claiming he wrote to fill his days. That it was his hobby, and that he was so good at it, he had to keep at it.

Total poseur.

Hugh clapped his hands together. "So, Lill, tell me about yourself. What are you working on now? Bert tells me you're a great writer."

Wow. Just wow.

"I have one finished romance novel, and another in the works. Hugh, are you really trying to get into the romance market?"

He gave me a big, phony smile. God, he was a bigger douche than I'd even thought.

"Oh yeah. Romance is the future of publishing. It's perennially popular, and there's so much great material out there that needs to get in front of readers."

Someone had just read the recent article in *Publisher's Weekly*.

Plain and simple, he was grotesque.

"You're right, Hugh. It's true."

It was absolutely true, only this asshole had no idea what he was talking about. What did he think, that by flattering me, I'd pull my panties down and bend over for him?

"So tell me this, Lill. How much sex do your books have?"

Interesting question to lead with.

"Well, quite a bit."

The pen he'd been twirling in his fingers tumbled out of his grip and to the floor. He didn't seem to notice.

He swallowed. "Oh. Really?" he asked in a quiet

voice. His face grew very serious, and he shifted in his seat.

Was he…?

No. No way.

"Well, um, can you tell me how much sex? And what kind of sex?"

What? Was he kidding?

"Hugh, if you read my book you'll see."

He nodded, as if to admit I had a point. "You're right. But I've only gotten into the first few pages. So maybe you can give me an… um… snapshot."

Oh for Christ's sake.

"There are several sex scenes," I said.

His eyes widened. "Really? Oh, that's great. Really great," he mumbled, his gaze not wavering from mine.

He shifted again.

Jesus. Was the creep getting a hard-on?

Figures he was friends with Bert.

"You know, Lill, I could probably give you some ideas."

He attempted a weak smile.

"Ideas? Like for getting published?" I knew damn well that's not what he meant. But I was going to make him work.

He half-laughed half-choked. "No, no that's not what I mean. I'm talking about giving you ideas for your sex scenes. For your um, books." He swallowed.

"Well, thanks, Hugh. But I don't need ideas for sex scenes."

I'd had enough. I stood and leaned onto his desk so he had to look up at me. "I come up with plenty of my own hot, dirty sex scenes, Hugh. Sometimes they involve two girls and a guy, sometimes two guys and a girl, sometimes oral and anal. So I think I've got all the good stuff covered, don't you?"

His eyes widened and he peered up at me. I wasn't sure whether he was terrified or turned on. Or both. "Oh. Right. Sure, Lill."

I pulled my bag up on my shoulder. "I think I'll be getting to work now, Hugh. Thanks for the super informative meeting."

He started to stand, but looked down at his lap and decided against it.

So. Gross.

"Okay, Lill, we'll keep in touch. I've always wanted to get to *know* a romance writer."

Jesus Christ.

I reached in my purse, and came back with a tissue, which I threw at him. "Here ya go, Hugh. Use this when you jerk off thinking about me and my sex scenes. Because that's the closest you're going to get to us, imagining them in your little pea brain."

His mouth dropped open.

And he took the tissue.

CHAPTER 28

Lill

"Hey, how'd your meeting go with the agent guy?" Cal asked at the end of another long day.

Dex served us drinks in his amazing living room, and then joined us, plopping down into a comfy leather chair. He'd offered to have Chinese brought in and Cal and Thorn said yes so fast I got swept up in the enthusiasm, probably ordering way more than I could possibly eat.

"Oh that. Well, it didn't go, let's put it that way," I said, staring out Dex's window at the twinkling city lights. "He was basically just hitting on me."

Thorn snorted. "Can't blame the bastard for that," he said, laughing.

I gave him the stink eye. Sure, he'd meant it as a compliment, but I was not in the mood.

"Well, that's too bad," Cal said. "I'm sorry."

"Yeah, baby. Hang in there. Just when you least expect it, something will open up for you and it will be amazing," Thorn added.

I forced a small smile. They really were nice men.

Nice in all sorts of ways. And I didn't mean just to look at.

The way they took their jobs so seriously, and wanted to keep me safe, was something I'd initially taken for granted.

I'd thought they were overzealous, exaggerating the threats against the von Malsens—and me—way out of proportion.

But the more time I spent with them and understood what they did and how, the more I realized they weren't being cautious because they had nothing better to do. They didn't particularly relish putting themselves in harm's way, and their goal was to mitigate that danger as much as possible.

And they were so goddamn hot, too.

The delivery guy arrived not a moment too soon because I was freaking starving. Evidenced by the way the guys dug into the bags of food, I was not the only one.

I sank my chopsticks into thick, oily lo mein noodles and aimed them in my mouth. "Mmmm," I moaned. It had been too long since I'd had good Chinese food.

Thorn's mind immediately went to dirty. "You'd better not moan like that, baby. You'll give me ideas."

Well. That didn't sound like such a bad thing.

I set my food down on the coffee table. "What do you mean, Thorn?" I asked coyly.

It took him about a nanosecond to realize I was flirting.

He set his food down, too. "Baby. When you do that shit, my dick starts to get hard."

Right to the point. That was our Thorn.

Cal and Dex looked at each other, chuckling.

What the fuck. It had been a day.

Walking over, I stopped right in front of him. "How hard, Thorn?"

I was going for it and there was no stopping me.

I ran my hands over the shaved sides of his head until I reached his ponytail, which I wove my fingers through. That was when I saw, possibly for the first time, past the veneer of Thorn the bad boy and into the tender gaze of a man who knew what it was like to be knocked down. And who knew the importance of getting back up.

The unexpected connection drew me to his lips.

"Damn, look at that," Dex said from behind me.

"Yo. Come on over and get some for yourself, Dex," Thorn mumbled, returning to our kiss. He stood, gripping my hair and tilting my head back to kiss me harder.

Dex's hands wrapped around me from behind, cupping my breasts and running his thumbs over my hard nipples. He unbuttoned my blouse and let it fall to the floor while Thorn opened my jeans and pushed them down my legs.

I stepped out of my Chucks and the tangle of clothes hanging off my body until I stood there in a lacy pink thong and matching bra.

Thank god I'd listened to Beebie's advice about wearing my good underwear. *Why save it?* she'd always asked.

Cal, still seated across the room, gave a low whistle.

"What are you doing over there by yourself?" I hummed, running my hands over my breasts.

"Mmmm," he said quietly.

Suddenly my feet were no longer on the ground. Thorn picked me and laid me back on the sofa. Positioning himself between my legs, he pried aside the lace crotch of my thong and ran a finger through my soaked pussy.

"Damn," he groaned.

"Let me have some," Dex said, running his own finger through my lips. "Baby's wet for us, guys."

Holy fuck. Something about these guys, in charge and taking what they wanted while making sure I got what I wanted, was intoxicating.

I felt so cared for. And safe.

And any thoughts about the shitty parts of my life were so far from my consciousness it was as if they didn't exist.

Thorn knelt between my legs and tongued me from bottom to top, circling my clit and creating a suction that had me writhing. At the same time, Dex lowered himself to slide his cock into my mouth. Cal was watching from behind the sofa, and with my free hand, I reached up, fumbling with his belt and fly until I could grip his hard cock.

Me and the guys. Amazing.

Dex fucked my mouth while Thorn continued to suck my clit. He slipped one finger in my pussy and then another in a delicious, slow motion. When he pulled them back out, he pressed one against my ass. Before I could panic, he slipped it easily inside. With a finger in my ass, he put another in my pussy, and continued working my clit.

I was in heaven. Complete and total ecstasy.

"Fuck, baby, I'm gonna come," Dex growled, pumping my mouth. "Can you take it?"

"Mmmm," was all I could say. But my inability to speak was compensated by gripping his balls to pull him deeper into my mouth.

In moments, my throat was flooded with his cum, which I did my best to swallow. He pulled out while still spurting, covering my breasts with the rest of it.

Thorn increased the speed with which he was finger fucking me when an orgasm hit me like a truck.

I closed my eyes and my mind went blank. I was nothing more than sensation and reflex as my body bucked out of control.

I was hungry—no, actually starving—for everything these guys gave me and only wanted more. As soon as Thorn took his fingers out of me, I flipped over on the sofa, kneeling. I didn't say a thing as I pushed my ass in the air.

I didn't need to.

The guys shuffled behind me and I heard a condom unrolling just before someone positioned himself at my opening.

"You ready, baby?" Cal growled, smoothing his hands over my ass cheeks.

"Mmmm. Yes, Cal," I said, trying to push back on him.

"Fuck her, dude. Do it," Thorn said, pushing my head down on the sofa.

I thrust myself back toward Cal at the same time he entered me. We both groaned, and rubbing my clit, I orgasmed again almost instantly. With my face in the sofa, I gasped for air.

But I didn't care.

Everything was perfect as I floated through post-orgasmic bliss.

I wasn't sure how much time had passed but Dex eventually wrapped me up in his huge bathrobe. I ate a couple more bites of my lo mein, but was so out of it I couldn't stop smiling.

"Darlin'," Thorn said, "we have something to talk to you about. An offer."

"Yeah?" I said dreamily. There was nothing they could offer me that was better than that moment. I seriously wanted time to stop.

"We want to share you. As in all three of us date you."

What? What the hell did that mean?

"Can we talk about it tomorrow," I murmured, my eyes falling closed. I was in no shape to make any life decisions.

One of the guys kissed me on the temple, I wasn't sure which.

"Of course, baby. Of course."

CHAPTER 29

Dex

I couldn't help myself.
The von Malsens were having a party. I was working security. And I couldn't keep my eyes off the damn front door.

I was waiting for Lill to come in.

It turned out that rich people invited their interior designers to their parties, I guess to trot them out and tell everyone 'look what I can afford.' And the designers themselves were eager to come because, who knows, they might meet new clients.

Lill had let us know her roommate Beebie—the von Malsens' decorator—had invited her to come along as her plus-one. I hadn't said anything, but I wasn't convinced Amalia wanted her cleaning lady as a guest at her ritzy party. But if Lill had the balls to show up, more power to her.

That's one of the things I liked about our girl.

She hadn't hesitated for a second to get down and dirty with us guys the other night at my house. And damn if she wasn't sexy as hell with all the sucking and fucking—

"Yay, there's my decorator. Beebie! You're here!" Amalia cried, as if she were meeting a long lost friend.

She teetered across the room in her skyscraper heels, engulfing Beebie in her arms. When she finally let go and took a step back, she spotted Lill, who stood there smiling and just generally being a goddamn knockout.

Seriously. I knew I was biased, but she blew all the other women at the party straight out of the water with her looks.

Like I knew she would.

And Amalia wasn't happy about that. Not at all. The smile slipped from her face like butter off a hot pan.

Was she going to be gracious? Or a bitch?

I put my money on bitch.

Amalia's now-regretful outburst had not attracted the room's attention quite the way she'd hoped. Instead of everyone admiring her choice in decorators, all eyes were now on Lill.

It wasn't hard to see why.

My girl wore a slim, black halter dress that hugged

her curves like it was made for her. It narrowed all the way down her thighs, where it stopped just below her knees.

The contrast of the black against her pale skin was breathtaking, as was the pile of messy red hair artfully arranged at her neck. It was the perfect casual counterpoint to the almost-severe dress she was rocking.

Hot damn. I wanted to take a picture, as did every other guy at the party. But little did they know, she'd probably be going home with *me*.

Probably. I never assumed.

And that made me infinitely pleased.

"Beebie, Lill, so nice to see you. And you ladies are stunning tonight, I might add," Eckie said effusively, kissing each on the cheek.

Christ, how did he end up with that horrible wife?

Amalia took Beebie by the arm as if Lill weren't even there, and escorted her into the party for introductions.

Lill's smile faltered for a moment until Beebie turned to her, interrupting Amalia, and beckoned for her to follow.

"Do you have any champers, Amalia? Lill and I would love a glass."

Fuck. That Beebie was a baller. She didn't miss a damn thing.

Amalia's face darkened, but she waved over a server.

Just then, Robbie came running down the stairs in his Superman pajamas, his nanny close on his heels.

"Here's my baby boy," Amalia cried. "Coming to say night-night to everyone. Show our friends your good manners, Robbie."

In a surprising display of self-control, Robbie started to whiz through the room shaking random peoples' hands.

"Hello, hello, hello," he repeated to each person in the loud voice of a six-year-old.

Until he got to Lill.

Looking her up and down, he scrunched up his face. "Lill, why do you look so weird?"

She laughed, as did everyone else. "You don't like my dress, Robbie?" she said, trying not to smile.

He just shrugged and moved on to the next grown up.

After several introductions, and with a champagne glass in hand, Lill left Beebie and wandered over to me.

"Oh my god. That kid is too funny," she said, shaking her head.

I lowered my voice. "That was funny as shit. He's never seen you without your jeans and sneakers."

She lifted her glass to me and sighed. "Wish you could join me," she said with a smile.

I stepped close to her ear and lowered my voice. "I don't need a drink, baby. All I want to do is look at you."

She titled her head, gazing at me, and a light blush

spread over her face. Fuck, I liked that. A beautiful woman who was also modest.

Didn't get much better than that.

I gestured toward the party. "Go ahead, darlin'. Mingle. I'm supposed to be working."

But before she did, Amalia showed up. "Lill, I didn't know you were coming, but now that you're here, can you pick up some of the empty glasses scattered about?"

Oh no she didn't.

This could get ugly.

But Lill was a champ about it. "Sure, Amalia," she said. "Shall we do it together?"

Amalia's mouth dropped open. "Oh. Um. Yes of course." She picked up one glass and headed for the kitchen.

Big of her.

God, I wanted to burst out laughing. The bitch had just gotten a taste of her own medicine.

I wouldn't have minded telling the couple dudes staring at Lill's ass as she picked up empty wine glasses to back the fuck off. I could be a little overprotective that way.

And when I followed Lill into the kitchen, my own gaze was glued to her pretty derriere.

"Still glad you came?" I asked.

"Oh sure. What the hell," she said, laughing.

"Wanna meet me in the stairwell out back?" she

asked, looking me up and down with a naughty twinkle.

"Fuck yeah, baby," I said, adjusting myself in my trousers. "You go first. I'll take a lap and then meet you."

She giggled. When she was sure no one was looking, she disappeared through the laundry room and out the apartment's back door.

CHAPTER 30

Dex

I did a quick scan of the party, where most of the women stood in a gaggle talking about their Botox treatments, and the men stood on the other side talking about business and current events.

It was a well-dressed crowd attending a boring-ass party on the Upper East Side. No more, no less.

"Hey, where's Lill?" Beebie asked me quietly when she was going for a refill.

"Um, she's in the stairwell. Waiting for me," I said devilishly,

Beebie broke out in a huge smile. "Well, don't keep her waiting," she whispered, and returned to the party.

I couldn't have kept her waiting if I'd wanted to. That's how badly I needed to run my hand over the smooth fabric hugging her ass.

"Hey, you," she said, when I'd sneaked out.

I took her hand. "C'mon. Let's walk down half a floor."

It was the perfect place to rendezvous. If anyone came looking for us, which I doubted they would, or had to take the trash to the chute, which I suspected Amalia was saving for Lill, we'd hear them coming.

In her stiletto heels, Lill was nearly eye-to-eye with me, a first since I usually saw her in sneakers.

Or nothing at all.

"Baby, do you know how fucking hot you look? Every man in the place was checking you out."

"Oh, I don't know about that, but I can say with certainty the moment I laid eyes on you when we arrived, I started to feel a little naughty." She looked at me boldly. "I know we should wait till later, but I just didn't think I could."

She wasn't kidding. Her fingers went straight for my pants. In seconds I was standing in the stairwell with my naked ass hanging out for the world to see.

And my hard dick in Lill's mouth.

She'd taken a seat on the steps, and with me at the perfect height for her pretty mouth, sucked me with vigor. Without missing a beat, she pulled my cock out of her mouth and began to tongue my balls while stroking my erection. I put one hand on the stairwell railing to remain upright, and pulled her head closer.

"Goddamn, baby, look at you. Are you trying to make me explode?"

She looked up at me. "Maybe."

She went back to my dick, taking me as deep in her throat as she could while cradling my balls in her hand.

Holy fuck, I wasn't going to last long at this rate. I pulled myself out of my girl's mouth and reached into my pants for a condom.

"Turn around," I told her.

When she did, I shimmied her dress up over her hips, and bent her forward until she was holding the steps right in front of her.

"You're not wearing panties, Lill," I scolded, lightly smacking her ass.

I sheathed myself, and pointed my dick at her wet pussy.

"Oops. Must have forgotten," she giggled, reaching back and holding my tip at her entrance.

"Are you ready for me, baby?" I asked.

"Yes, Dex. Please fuck me." She wagged her ass for emphasis.

That's my girl.

I plunged into her up to my balls. I knew I wasn't going to last long, but I was dying to feel her come on my cock.

A low moan escaped her lips, and I knew she was going to come fast, just like me.

"God yes, Dex. Give it to me," she murmured.

I fucked her like I'd wanted to fuck her all night, urgently pumping her pussy until I knew it would be sore. She pounded her fists on the stairs, her head bucking, the only sounds from her mouth guttural and primal. And hungry.

God, what that woman did to me.

"Here it comes, baby," I groaned, and thrust just in time for her to come so hard I wondered if I'd have to carry her back to the party.

I unloaded deep inside her, and although I was so spent my legs were quivering, I knew I had to go back to work. I grabbed the condom, knotted it, and pulled Lill's dress back down while she tucked loose strands of hair back into the nest at the base of her neck.

"Nice move, going commando."

She smoothed a couple small wrinkles out of her dress and smiled. "Are you complaining?"

Was she fucking kidding?

After I'd put myself back together, I took her hand and we went back up the stairwell. "Let me go in first. Follow me in a minute or two."

"Okay, bossy security guy," she said.

I kissed her temple, wishing we had time for more, and quietly opened the apartment's back door. Fortunately, the kitchen was empty save for the hired server, who I wasn't worried about. I made my way to back to the party, which had about doubled in size since Lill and I left.

Amalia and Eckie were busy with their friends. No one had noticed us missing. Beebie winked at me from across the room, and I had to look away to keep from laughing. As I did, Lill joined the party. With her sights set on Beebie, she began to work her way across the room. But she stopped in her tracks, her eyes widening. She turned on her heel and ran back to the kitchen.

What the hell was that?

I looked around, and finding nothing out of the ordinary, followed her. "Hey. Are you okay?"

She clutched her purse, shaking. "Dex. I have to get out of here."

"Why? What's wrong?"

"Did you see the man Amalia's talking to?" she asked.

I stuck my head around the kitchen door. On the other side of the room, Amalia held the attention of a young man.

But she was doing more than talking. She was standing close. Very close. Much closer that you would for a normal conversation. And she was twirling her hair with her finger.

"Whoa. You mean the dude she's flirting with?" I asked.

She wasn't even hiding it.

I looked into the living room again. Christ, she was really working it. And Eckie was on the other side of the room, oblivious.

Wow.

Lill nodded, heading toward the back door. "That's the guy... the guy who tried to grab Robbie," she said in a trembling voice. "I saw his face that day. I'll never forget it."

Her panicked eyes filled with tears.

Holy shit. What the hell was he doing here, at the von Malsens' party?

But I didn't have time to think about that. Lill's safety was my top priority.

I steered her toward the door. "We need to get you out of here. Wait in the stairwell. I'll be right out."

I returned to the party and snapped a photo of the guy Amalia was all over. I forwarded it to Cal and Thorn and joined Lill where I'd fucked her only moments earlier.

"C'mon," I said, taking her hand, and of course, checking my gun.

As soon as we hit the street, I hailed a cab that took us to Regulator. As we rushed in the front door, Jen looked up from the drink she was mixing. She looked at me with an *is everything all right?* expression.

I looked back and her and shook my head, pulling Lill through the crowded bar to the door that led to our small office, where she sank into an old wooden chair.

"Go ahead and text Beebie. Tell her you left, but don't alarm her."

In the meantime, my own phone was blowing up with texts from Amalia, looking for me.

Fuck.

Moments later, a message came in from Cal.

we have to take Lill to the cabin. now

CHAPTER 31

Lill

I leaned over the trashcan in Dex's office just in time to be sick.

"Oh my god. I'm sorry," I whispered, shaking so hard I couldn't move.

"Baby, don't apologize. Here's a paper towel. Let me get you some water."

I reached for him. "No. Please don't leave me, Dex."

He hesitated. "Just let me wave out the door for Jen. She'll help."

Lovely. Puking in front of the ultra-hot guy I'd just had sex with.

Jen brought me water a minute later. Tiny sips of it were soothing going down, and I immediately felt better. Dex dabbed my forehead with some of the water using a paper towel, and I wanted to cry, it felt that good.

Holy shit. Thank god he was at the party with me. And thank god he was with me at that very moment.

I didn't think of myself as a clingy, simpering female, but at that moment, all I wanted to do was hang on him.

He was a protector. He was *my* protector.

"You feeling better?" he asked.

In some regards yes, but in others, no.

"If you're asking whether I'm going to barf again, the answer is no. But I'm not sure how positive that is given the current state of the rest of my life." I dropped my head into my hands.

"Sorry, baby," he said, rubbing my back. "I know it sucks."

Fuck. How in god's name did I get involved with whatever shitty drama the von Malsens had going on, anyway? To begin with, I never even should have been with Robbie that day someone tried to snatch him. How the hell had Amalia's nanny problems become mine?

And why was I working for that horrible woman, who left her dirty underpants on the floor? Who does that?

I shouldn't have gone to their party. Beebie had insisted on bringing me, saying it would be fun. An excuse to dress up. Maybe meet some interesting people.

Yeah. Should have stayed home with my Ben & Jerry's.

I looked up, squinting to ward off the headache circling my brain. "Dex, what was that man doing there? It makes no sense. He tried to kidnap their *child*. Do you think they know?"

Or did they have no idea?

He pressed his lips together, and looked at his phone. "Cal and Thorn will be here in a minute. Let's hold on for them to get here."

Fine. I felt relatively safe. But what about Robbie? What about the von Malsens? Was that man going to try and make off with one of them?

Just then, Cal and Thorn burst in.

Thorn knelt next to me and took my hand. "Are you okay, baby?"

The worried expression on his normally tough-guy face did something to me. My shoulders started heaving, and the sobs came, at first silent and then loud and hard.

But instead of acting like I was a crazy bitch and running away like most guys would, Thorn stayed by my side, holding my hand and occasionally bringing it to his lips for a kiss. He was *with* me on this fucked up journey, and that said everything about his character.

After several minutes of purging myself of the fear,

frustration, and anger that pushed me to a breaking point, I realized Cal and Dex were making a plan.

"What... what are you guys talking about? What are we going to do?" I asked, blowing my nose.

"Lill, can you remember ever seeing that guy anywhere else besides the time he tried to grab Robbie?" Cal asked, frowning.

I shook my head. "No. If I had, I would have remembered him and told you guys."

With his hands on his hips, he looked down at his shoes. "Well, he's clearly in the von Malsens' circle of acquaintances. This is not comforting."

Dex shook his head. "Dude, he was no acquaintance. Amalia was practically tearing her clothes off for him right there at the party. There is no doubt in my mind they have something going on."

Could that have something to do with the condom I'd found in Amalia's things?

"Fine. Maybe he's even their friend. I'm heading over to the von Malsens' now. I'll tell them you got sick, Lill, that Dex took you home, and that he called me to take over."

"What about me? What am I going to do?" I asked.

"You're going to the cabin. It's the only place you'll be safe tonight. We don't know if the guy at the party saw you, or whether he was there looking for you. But he's clearly bad news and we need some answers."

Shit. Not the cabin.

It was one thing to go up there for the day. That was

fine. Actually awesome, considering the fun I'd had with Cal and Thorn. But to stay up there?

No. Sorry.

"Cal, I can't do that. I'm not going up to the cabin. I don't want to stay there."

He knelt in front of me and took my hands. "It's not forever, Lill. But we are paid by Eckie to keep you safe. We don't know for sure yet who the good guys and bad guys are, and until we do, we can't take any chances with you. If anything happened…"

His voice cracked, and he looked away.

Holy shit. He was really afraid.

"Please, Lill. I couldn't live with myself," he pleaded.

"Hear, hear," Dex said in agreement.

Well, shit. Way to pull the guilt card.

He stood and turned to Thorn. "Here are the keys to my SUV and the cabin. I'll be in touch as soon as I can." He gave me a hard kiss on the lips, and left.

I buried my head in my hands. "How can I go up there? I don't have any stuff."

"That's the least of your worries, darlin'," Thorn said. "There are clothes at the house you can wear until we take you into town tomorrow to get what you need."

"Beebie will be worried. And what do I tell Amalia about my job? I can't just quit."

Dex pulled me to my feet. "C'mon. We need to hit the road. But you certainly can quit. Those people have almost gotten you killed more than once. I think it's time to tell the von Malsens goodbye."

What? Was he crazy? Did he think I had some big inheritance waiting for me somewhere? I mean, I would love to say goodbye to my cleaning job, Amalia, and her unruly child. But it just wasn't a viable option.

"You don't understand, Dex. I need that job, shitty as it may be."

He sighed patiently. "Lill, do you know anything about how I got my condo downtown?"

Didn't he just buy it like most people did?

"How? From your earnings here at the bar?"

He laughed, running his hand along the shaved sides of his head. "Not exactly, baby. Running a bar like this would not have permitted me to buy any condo, much less the one I'm living in right now. My place was very, very expensive, not only because it looks cool, but because of the security it offers."

I frowned at him? Was he a drug dealer, too?

No, Cal would not have hired a drug dealer.

"Wh… where did you get your money from, Dex?"

"I was in private security for years. It's very lucrative. Extremely lucrative, actually. I did my years with the firm, and I was rewarded for it."

So he was loaded?

As if he read my mind, he nodded. "Yeah. Now you're putting two and two together. The money I made not only bought me that apartment, but also this bar."

"You didn't get rich from the bar?" I asked.

He laughed again. "No. The bar is kind of a hobby job. It's something to do. I don't even pay myself. But I pay my workers well. That's why I can take a chunk of time off to help Cal with a special project like this."

Okay. Fine. The guy was loaded. What did that have to do with my shitty cleaning job?

"Like we told you, Lill, we guys want to date you. We *all* want to date you. Share you. And until you get on your feet with a real job, I can support you," he said.

Oh god no. Just what I needed, to be indebted to some guy.

I looked over at Thorn.

He nodded. "It's a good offer, darlin'. Think about it," he said. "It would take worrying about money off the table, if only for a little while."

"Thorn's right, Lill. Think about it. You don't have to make any decisions tonight. Or even tomorrow. We're not going anywhere."

They helped me to my feet.

"Well, we *are* going somewhere, right now," I said with a weak laugh.

I had to find some humor in the situation. Otherwise, I'd start crying again.

CHAPTER 32

Lill

The entire two-hour drive up to the cabin, I'd been wracking my brains trying to remember how many bedrooms the place had.

Had it been two or three?

Or, worse, only one?

And if that were the case, what would the sleeping arrangements be?

Shit.

And what was this *sharing* business that kept coming up?

Like, would I be with all three guys? Or pick one?

I was so confused.

I couldn't be with three men. Who does that?

When we arrived, Dex and Cal said it was okay to make a quick call to Beebie.

"Hey, I won't be home for a few days," I said.

I heard her moving around the apartment, most likely getting ready for bed. "Oooh, sounds like fun. Too bad you missed the rest of the party."

Yeah. The cabin was super fun. As the party had been.

I was dying to tell her what was going on, but the guys had pointed out that the less she knew, the safer she was.

"Yeah. It will be great. So what happened at the party after I left?" I asked, grabbing the attention of Dex and Thorn.

"Oh god," Beebie said with a long sigh. "Amalia was flirting up a storm with some friend of Eckie's. It was so embarrassing."

My stomach dropped. "Oh really? I hadn't noticed," I said in a shaky voice, switching my phone to speaker and waving the guys over. "Do you know who he was?" I asked.

"Oh yeah. Some finance guy. Or supposed finance guy. There are a lot of rumors about him."

"Like what?" I asked.

Beebie's bed creaked in the background. I'd better ask my questions fast, because when she was in bed, she was done for the night.

"I don't know a lot. Just like he lost some of his clients' money. Stuff like that. But Amalia convinced him to hire me to decorate his place. You'd better believe I'm getting a cash deposit from him if he has money problems." She laughed.

Always the good businesswoman.

"Cool, Beebie. I'm sure you'll do a great job for him. And what's his name?"

She sighed. "Brandon. Brandon Yates."

"Brandon Yates," I repeated, and Thorn texted it to Cal. "I don't know him."

"Well, no big loss. I personally find him kind of douche-y. I mean last time I met with him he was asking me all kinds of information about my financials. At first I thought he wanted me to invest with him. But then he started hitting on me so hard, I got the feeling like he was looking for a sugar momma. Crazy, right?"

Yeah. Crazy. It was all crazy.

After finishing with Beebie, Dex told me to choose a bedroom out of the cabin's two. Thorn would take the other and Dex would be on the sofa.

"Here are some sweats and a T-shirt. I think that will be fine for tonight?" Dex asked.

I nodded. "Hey, how is it you guys know your way around here so well?"

They looked at each other. "This is where we train. Cal hires people to act out a whole variety of the situations we could potentially face working security, so we can keep our skills sharp."

Holy shit. I had no idea.

"God. You guys are real pros."

Thorn shrugged. "Did you think you were dealing with amateurs, baby?" he asked, laughing.

"Good night. If you need anything, we'll just be in the next room," Dex said, pulling my door closed.

Well. I was glad they hadn't assumed I'd be sleeping with one or both of them. After the stresses of the night, sexy was the last thing I was feeling, and an assumption that I'd be automatically available would have only pissed me off.

They probably felt the same.

CHAPTER 33

Thorn

I was wrenched out of a deep sleep with someone's hands grabbing my shoulders.

I'd been trained for this shit, and sprang into action.

Without thinking, I reached into the dark and pulled them into a choke hold with my left arm, and grabbed the gun from under my pillow with my right, clicking off the safety and pressing the barrel to their temple.

I hesitated for a moment before shooting their brains out with what I considered to be a very generous warning.

"Stop right there," I growled.

The intruder instantly froze in my grip, whimpering quietly.

"No… wait… Thorn, stop. It's me. Please."

Horrified, I let go. In the dark room, I watched the silhouette of Lill tumble onto the floor next to my bed.

Lill? The intruder was Lill? What the hell was she doing grabbing my shoulders in the middle of the night?

Was she goddamn insane?

I reached for the nightstand light, switching the gun safety back on. "Jesus fucking Christ, girl. You know how close you just came to having your head shot off?"

She looked at me in horror. Jesus, she had a lot to learn.

"I… I'm… sorry. I didn't know…"

She scrambled to her feet and ran for the door.

"Wait," I barked.

She stopped, looking back at me.

The fear in her eyes—her fear of *me*—gutted my insides. The last thing I wanted was for my lovely girl to be afraid of *me*.

I was her goddamn protector.

I jumped out of bed but didn't rush her. I'd scared the shit out of her. I knew to take my time coaxing her back to a calm state.

I held my hands up. "I'm so sorry, baby. I didn't know it was you and just reacted the way I always would when on alert. Anyone of us would have done the same."

She just stared at me, horrified.

Which about broke my heart.

"Can you come here, darlin'? Sit on the bed next to me and talk?"

She stared as she inched closer, as if I'd pull the gun back out, and sat a couple feet away, hands in her lap.

Shit. I'd done a number on her.

"Baby, why'd you come in here? What's going on?" I asked.

I lightly ran my hand down the back of her sweatshirt hoping it would bring her back to me.

"I feel so stupid, Thorn. I'm sorry."

I inched closer and gently turned her face toward mine. "You have nothing to be sorry for. You didn't know how dangerous it was to wake one of us that way."

"Well, what should I have done?" she asked.

Why hadn't we gone over this before? It was basic security protocol.

Probably because I'd been spending a lot of time thinking with my little head.

"You could either knock on the door, or just open it and call me from across the room. A real intruder would not do that."

She laughed. "I guess not."

"So now are you gonna tell me why you were in here?"

She shrugged. "I heard an animal outside. It scared me."

Oh, for Christ's sake. I bit my tongue to keep from laughing.

"You think it's funny?" she asked, catching my smirk.

I shook my head hard. "No. Sorry. Did it sound kind of like a dog?" I asked.

Her eyes widened. "It did. How did you know?"

I took her hand and pulled her closer. She looked so small in the huge sweats we'd given her to sleep in, and her hair was a matted mess.

And she was still beautiful.

"It was a coyote, Lill. The woods around here are full of them. He was just howling to find his mate."

Not that different from a dude, if you thought about it.

She put her head in her hand. "Seriously? That's all it was?"

"Hey," I said, pulling her closer, "you know how happy it makes me that you came to me?"

She burrowed her head into my chest and wrapped her arms around me. "Really? You don't think I'm an idiot?"

I pulled back to look directly at her. "What? How could I think you're an idiot?"

Just then, another coyote howled in the distance.

"See? They're finding each other."

She looked up at me and smiled. "Can I stay in here with you tonight?"

Cripes. She had to even ask?

"'Course darlin'," I said, pulling back the covers on the other side of the bed and switching the light off.

Say what you want about the cabin, but Cal had put decent sheets, pillows, and comforters on the beds. Dex had complained bitterly after the first time we'd come up, and had shamed him into going to Target for new stuff.

It had actually been kind of funny, watching them bicker. Dex, I guess because of his cash windfall, was used to the finer things in life. Cal couldn't give a shit.

As for myself, I was just happy to have a bed to sleep in. And thanks to Cal, I was now sharing mine with one of the most fucking awesome women I'd ever met.

Not that there was usually a shortage of women in my life. In fact, one of my regular friends with benefits had stopped by just the week before. She was a hottie with great tits and a huge ass—just my jam—but I had to send her away. No one was more shocked than I was.

She'd immediately picked up on the fact that I'd met someone. And bless her, she was happy for me.

Lill snuggled under the covers, inching toward me, just as I'd hoped she might.

Who knew if either of us was going to be in the mood after my nearly shooting her head off? But it seemed we'd gotten past that.

Thank god.

I ran my hand up her shirt and over her heated skin

to find her breasts. I cupped one, running my fingers over its erect nipple, teasing just enough to make her gasp.

Which, of course, resulted in my semi-erect cock going full on hard.

"Jesus, baby, what you do to me," I said, pulling her to me for a kiss.

It was so mellow, lying there on our sides, facing each other with coyotes howling off and on like wild background music.

"You feeling better now? A bit calmer?" I asked, pushing the hair out of her face.

With a small amount of moonlight in the room, I could just make out her nodding head.

"Yes, thank you."

I went back to kissing her delightful lips while running a hand down her back and into her sweatpants to grip her curvy ass. She scooted closer, and my hard on bounced against her thigh.

"Oh. My," she teased.

My ass she was surprised. She knew very well what she did to me.

"Baby got my dick hard," I said. "Again."

She abruptly sat up, pulling off her sweats. There was my beautiful girl, smooth, naked, and luscious.

"Fuck baby, you're bare down there," I said, running my fingers through her wet pussy.

"Yeah. Finally had time for a wax," she laughed.

Damn.

She pushed the covers off the bed and knelt over me, throwing my boxers to the floor. Positioning herself between my legs, she took hold of my cock and interlacing her fingers around it, stroked up and down my shaft with both hands.

Holy fuck. This woman was goddamn amazing. And in the moonlight, I could only see her perfect outline.

"Damn, Lill, that feels awesome." I lay back on my pillow and closed my eyes, enjoying her soft hands.

I never thought I'd be experiencing this in Cal's little weekend getaway. It had only ever been guys here during my previous visits and having female energy in the place changed it completely.

Especially when said female was stroking my cock like a champ.

"Darlin' I think I need to be inside you," I said quietly.

"Oh yes," she whispered. "I think you do."

I reached for the pants I'd dropped onto the floor and fished through the pockets.

"Here. Cover me, baby."

Lill ripped open the plastic condom packet and sheathed me in seconds. Then she placed her legs on either side of my hips and hovered above my cockhead.

I reached in the dark, and held her open. She lowered herself slowly, very slowly, as she adjusted to my girth.

"Fuck, baby, that feels nice," I said when she wasn't even all the way down on me.

I was going to come quick. There was just no way around it.

"Mmmm," she moaned when she was fully seated on me.

She began rocking back and forth in small movements, and in the dark I could see her head begin to sway, swinging her hair back and forth. I gripped her hips, following her rhythm as my eruption grew closer.

I pulled her down toward me and with her tits pressed against my chest, held her tight as she ground harder, her breath ragged in my ear.

She gasped. "Fuck me, Thorn. I'm coming. Oh god."

That was all I needed to hear.

An explosion that started in my balls worked its way through me. I roared, coming so hard we nearly flew off the bed. "Fuck, baby, I'm coming," I bellowed.

Panting, she kept riding me until she was wiped out.

I helped her onto her back before I disposed of our condom.

I grabbed the covers off the floor where she'd thrown them and pulled them up and over us. Turning her to face away, spooning-style, I wrapped my arms around her and buried my nose in her sweet hair.

In the distance, another coyote howled. This time, my girl wasn't afraid.

I woke up with the sun, like I always did. I'd been a morning person all my life, and even when I was working the streets until three or four in the morning, I still got up early every damn day.

My beautiful girl continued to snooze with a couple little snores here and there. Her red hair sprayed across the white sheets and she was such a vision that it caused a pain in my chest.

Jesus, I was turning into a pussy.

It was just as well I woke up because it was my turn to make a lap around the property. Cal's cabin sat on a shit ton of acreage—how much I had no idea—but if you wanted, you could wander for hours. I wasn't going to be gone that long, but I knew where all the access points were and needed to make sure they were secure.

"Where're you going?" Lill murmured, rubbing her eyes.

I sat on her side of the bed, kissed her on the forehead, and pulled on my boots. "Gonna take a lap around. Security check. When I get back, we'll take you to town for some things."

"How do you know it's safe there?" she asked.

"We don't."

CHAPTER 34

Lill

"Jesus. Cal wants us to return to the city right now," Dex said, putting his phone down and turning the car around.

I leaned forward to get in on the front seat conversation. "What? Why? Right now? Like this?" I looked down at my oversized sweats and Cal's flipflops, which Thorn had shortened by cutting the backs off so I could walk without tripping.

"He's got a plan. And you're part of it, Lill."

Great. Just great. Now my life was going to be in even more danger than it already was.

Thanks, guys.

"You're going to be bait."

Oh my god.

"We're stopping at your place first so you can get cleaned up and changed into fresh clothes. Then, we're meeting at the Regulator office to hear the plan."

I don't think so.

"You know, guys, I'm not ready to go back. Can you just drop me at the cabin? It seems like a good place to chill out while I think about my life. Figure some things out. Go ahead and go back to the city without me. I'll wait up here at the cabin."

They looked at each other.

"No," Thorn said.

For Christ's sake.

These guys had dragged me up here, made me spend the night in Cal's crummy cabin—although it had turned out to be pretty freaking awesome, thanks to Thorn—and now they're bringing me back to use as bait?

This bullshit was getting out of control.

"Baby, why don't you want to go back?" Thorn asked, turning from the front seat to see me.

I folded and unfolded my hands. Nervous energy was making my skin crawl. "New York… is just not working out that well for me. I can't get the job thing off the ground, someone wants to kill me. Basic stuff like that."

"You know, New York gives everyone a kick in the ass every now and then. In fact, some of us get kicked on a regular basis." He looked out the window and laughed.

"What do you mean?" I asked.

"Well, my family was one of the last poor ones in Hell's Kitchen when it started being redeveloped. My dad refused to move until we were evicted. It just went downhill from there, and... let's just say my brother and I were not model children. But hard as it was, I left that shit behind. My point being, I made it work."

Yeah. Whatever.

"Damn, Lill, look at me," Dex said. "I had to leave college because I lost my scholarship. You know how devastating that was? But I ended up landing on my feet. I have a great home and a bar I love running. Make New York your bitch, Lill, not the other way around."

I didn't believe for a second that I was going to show New York who was boss like these two had, but their pep talks brought tears to my eyes.

"I guess I have a lot to think about," I said, watching the scenery whip by.

Not least of which was what I was doing messing around with three guys.

※ ※

Dex drove like a bat out of hell, and in barely over two hours I was clean and presentable, and in Regulator's office.

I hadn't watched the speedometer. I was afraid to.

"When will Cal be here?" I asked.

"Here I am," he said, flying into the room.

Now, maybe he'd finally tell us what the hell was going on.

"How was the cabin?" he asked.

Thorn pressed his lips together, and I looked down at my hands, trying to stifle a giggle.

We couldn't have been more obvious.

"It was great, Cal. That pullout sofa in your living room is a real gem," Dex said, rolling his eyes.

That did it. I laughed out loud.

"Well, it seems like two out of three people had fun. That's not so bad," he said with raised eyebrows, looking between Thorn and me.

Fun? That didn't begin to describe it.

"Here's what's up," he continued, getting serious. "The private investigator has confirmed that Brandon Yates and Amalia are having an affair. No big surprise there. She'd practically broadcast it at their party right under Eckie's nose."

I *knew* she was up to something.

My next thought was about poor Eckie. He was such a nice man.

"Okay. So, if that's the case, why would the guy she was having an affair with try to grab her kid?" I asked.

Cal pointed at me. "That's the big question. And I think I might know the answer. Beebie told you the guy was pretty much broke, right?"

I nodded.

Dex threw his arms up. "Holy shit. I know what they're up to."

Everyone turned toward him.

"What if Amalia was having Yates kidnap her kid for ransom money? That would give Yates the funds to get by on while she was getting ready to run out on Eckie."

Oh. My. God.

Were people really this diabolical?

Kidnap her own son to get money for the creep she's sleeping with? It was beyond disgusting.

"So she's known all along that I saw him, and he's been trying to get rid of me with her help ever since?" My voice caught.

Cal nodded. "I'm thinking that's why she sent you out with Robbie to begin with. She figured neither you nor I would be paying much attention. And when you saw Yates and could ID him, she had them wreck your apartment to scare the shit out of you. I bet they thought there'd be an opportunity to get rid of you at some point, too."

Holy shit. I'd been working for a truly evil person.

I leaned my head in my hands, and took long, deep breaths.

"I can't believe this. I just can't believe it," I mumbled.

"The whole story is fucking incredible," Thorn said,

revulsion washing over his face. "Did you tell Eckie anything yet?"

Cal looked down, sadly, and I knew the answer before he spoke. "Yeah. I had to. He was broken up, but he's a tough bastard. And I think he suspected something, on some level, anyway."

"So what's the plan?" Dex asked.

"That's what I was just getting to."

CHAPTER 35

Lill

It was clear to me now, in case it hadn't been before, that I was not the sort of person who should be involved in a sting operation. There was too much at stake, and I was inches away from losing my shit.

Eckie was at an event that night, and Amalia had let Cal know she had an 'engagement' of her own that she needed to be taken to.

An engagement, my ass.

We headed downtown to the gallery where she would be, and waited a block away in the car.

Fifteen minutes later, Cal texted us that he'd dropped her off.

Game on.

"Okay. I can do this," I told Dex and Thorn as I got out of the car.

I looked up and down the street, smoothing the wrinkles out of my clothes and fussing with my hair one last time. Gathering all the courage I could, I walked toward the gallery, which was buzzing with noise that could be heard from several doors down.

When I thought about it, I was sick and tired of being scared. What good was it doing me? Instead, I focused on how those assholes—Amalia and Yates—had fucked up my life. I was pissed, and getting more so, the closer I got to the gallery door.

Look out bitches. I was ready.

Holding my head high, I walked into the party. Sure, the crowd was good-looking and well dressed, but they were no better than me. I had just as much right to be there as they did. I was over being intimidated by New York.

It took only a moment to find Amalia on the other side of the room, of course canoodling with Yates. I ran through Cal's plan one more time, and pushed through the crowd.

"Lill? What are you doing here?" Amalia asked when she spotted me, her eyes wide. She disentangled herself from Yates and shifted uncomfortably. Her usual pleasant expression was anything but.

Yeah, lady, you'd better believe you've just been busted.

She glanced at Yates, who pressed his lips together and scanned the room.

Probably to assess how easy or difficult it would be to kill me.

But I was angry. And I held onto that like it was my lifeline.

I stretched up to my full height. "Amalia, do you realize this man you're with is the same one who tried to kidnap your son? And has been after me ever since, because I can identify him?"

Her mouth dropped open and just as she was about to speak, Yates took me by the upper arm, holding me in a grip I knew would leave bruises later.

"Shut up," he growled. "I have a gun. And I will use it. We're leaving now."

"Fuck you, creep," I said, trying to wrest my arm free.

When she realized Yates had gotten control of the situation, Amalia got in my face. "Lill, you had to be some sort of hero, didn't you? What did you think would happen, coming down here to confront us? You are such a stupid girl."

I leaned back at her, so close I could smell her expensive perfume. "Go fuck yourself, Amalia. Life as you know it is about to be over."

That's when I felt the butt of a gun pressing into my ribs. I looked down and saw Yates's hand deep in his pocket, where he must have hidden his weapon.

"Same for you, *Brandon Yates*," I hissed.

He glowered. "Shut the hell up and move toward the door. Slowly," he said.

That was enough. I'd played my part, and I wanted this fucker off me. I looked behind him and saw Cal heading our way with two police officers on his heels.

Blindsiding Yates, Cal swung the butt of his own gun against my captor's arm, causing him to stumble and let go of me. Cal grabbed his other arm, and twisted it behind his back. Yates's gun clattered to the floor, everyone around us gasping and giving us wide berth.

That was my clue to get the hell out of the way. I stepped behind Amalia as everyone in the gallery realized what was happening.

"Brendan Yates, you're under arrest for attempted kidnapping. And Amalia von Malsen, you're under arrest for aiding him."

Amalia looked around the room at the faces staring at her and laughed nervously as handcuffs were placed on her wrists. "Officer, there must be some sort of mistake. Please take these off me and we'll straighten it out. I had no idea this man tried to kidnap my little boy."

She looked at Yates with a mixture of shock and disgust.

She wasn't doing herself any favors.

"Fuck you, Amalia," Yates barked. "You think you can throw me under the bus? Think again."

"*You!*" Amalia screamed at me. "This is all your fault.

You've been trouble since the first day you started working for me. You should have just minded your own business."

God, I wanted to smack her stupid face.

"*You* and your boyfriend tried to kidnap your son. In what world is that not something only a sick fuck would do?" I yelled loudly enough for the entire gallery to hear.

And hear it they did. Shocked gasps fluttered through the crowd as people scurried to put some distance between the newly arrested criminals and themselves.

The cops led walked Amalia and Yates toward the door, the whispering crowd parting to let them through.

Cal slipped his hand into mine. "Good job, baby. You couldn't have done any better."

I looked up at Mister Security.

"Thank you Cal. Thank you for everything. Can we go home now?"

CHAPTER 36

Lill

I hadn't been in my apartment in a couple weeks and had almost forgotten what a mess it was from having been ransacked. But what had I expected? The place wasn't going to clean itself up.

"So, this is your crib?" Thorn asked, doing a three-sixty. "It's nice. You can put this back together in no time."

Dex nodded. "Cozy. I like it, too."

It was a cute apartment when it wasn't trashed. I shoved all the clothes lying around into a closet, and stacked the papers and books that had been strewn about onto a big easy chair.

Now that we knew who the bad guys were, it was

easy to figure out how they'd known where I lived and when I was coming and going.

"Ugh. What am I going to do with this apartment?" I mumbled.

"It's not really that bad, baby," Thorn said. He plopped down on the edge of my bed, making himself at home like he did everywhere he went.

"Why don't you come over here, gorgeous?" he asked with a wicked smile.

Fuck the apartment.

I sauntered over. "Why? What do you want, Thorn?" I asked coyly.

"I know what he wants," Dex said. "He wants to see you undressed. Just like I do."

I whirled around to face Dex. God, what these guys did to me.

It should be illegal.

"Is that right, Dex? Just like this?" I unzipped the back of my dress and let it fall to the floor in a puddle.

Cal whistled softly. "Turn around for us, baby."

Still in my high heels, and sheer panties and bra, I moved so they could see me from every angle.

And their admiring smiles were dizzying. They looked at me like I was the most beautiful woman in the world and for a moment, that's exactly how I felt.

Why were they so good to me? I sure as hell didn't do anything to deserve it.

Dex walked up behind me and ran his hands over my bra and down to my panties, where he slipped his hand inside and found my wet pussy. He pressed on my clit, and I pushed back against the erection restrained by his trousers.

"Fuck, you're wet," he murmured.

"What did you expect?" I laughed. "The three of you in my apartment all at once? Of course a girl's going to get excited."

"Lean back on the bed. I think I need to fuck you now," he growled.

His command sent a thrill through me and I promptly obeyed.

He dropped to his knees, pushing my legs apart. Running a finger up my slit, he brought it to my mouth for a taste.

"Do you like it?" he asked.

I took his fingers and sucked them clean, nodding since I couldn't speak.

"Guys, get on either side and hold her open for me."

Oh my god.

Thorn took my left leg and Cal my right, and pulled my legs back as far as they would go. I was completely exposed and I loved it. Dex did too, smiling at the view.

"Dex, please fuck me. I need you to fuck me."

"Music to my ears," he sang, pulling a condom out of his pocket.

When he'd sheathed himself, he held his hard cock at my opening. "Are you ready baby?"

"Yeah, Dex. Please. Please give it to me."

I gasped as he sank inside me. He was fucking huge

and it hurt at first, like it always did. But he held himself inside me, his gaze locked with mine, checking in to see how much I could take.

"Look at our girl," Dex said. "She's getting fucked by my big, fat cock."

Oh my god. These guys killed me.

He slipped slowly in and out and pushed a finger between my lips. "Get it wet, babe. Get my finger wet."

I sucked his finger into my mouth.

When it was wet, he pressed it against my asshole. I wiggled against him, and he pushed inside me. His big cock sliding in and out of my pussy, and the finger in my ass, was electrifying.

I grabbed Thorn and Cal on either side of me, and started to convulse as an orgasm shattered me. And shattered me again.

Holy shit. It wasn't stopping.

I thrashed my head back and forth on the bed, bucking my hips against Dex's invasion of my pussy and bottom.

"Oh god," was all I could murmur, over and over again.

Dex roared and I felt his length expand inside me, stretching my walls to the hilt. He exploded in a scary powerful orgasm. When he pulled out, Thorn and Cal released my legs and laid me down on the bed, covering me with my comforter. Dex took one side of the bed, and Cal the other. Thorn kicked off his shoes and lay down on my sofa.

Wow. Wow was all I could think. My thoughts were muddled as the guys snuggled me from both my right and left sides. I was safe, at last. I was protected.

Thanks to these guys.

My guys.

CHAPTER 37

Cal

"What are you so happy about today?"
Lill slid into the booth opposite me and waved Jen over for a beer.

She looked relaxed and happy, possibly for the first time since I'd met her in the von Malsens' foyer, when I'd patted her down.

That day had been funny as hell, though not for Lill. She'd been so hopping mad I had to struggle to keep from laughing. Seriously. Getting so indignant over something so trivial? But I'd keep that observation to myself.

"I have good news," she said, shimmying in her seat.

"But I'm waiting for the guys. Hey, want to hear something funny?" she offered.

"Always."

God, she was fucking adorable with her hair twisted into a messy braid and pulled forward over one shoulder, partially covering up her faded Rolling Stones T-shirt. It had only been hours since I'd been naked with her, and I was tempted to take her back into Dex's office that very moment.

But there'd be time for that later.

"So, back when I first started working for the von Malsens, I came in one morning and you were out in front of their building talking to a beautiful woman. I thought you had something going on with her and I was kind of pissed because you'd just kissed me."

Who was she referring to? I was talking to a woman outside the von Malsens'?

She read the confusion on my face. "Turns out, it was Jen's wife. You were talking to her about working for someone in the building."

Well, I'll be damned. She was jealous. I wouldn't have guessed it.

I reached across the table for her hand. "Silly girl," I said just as Dex and Thorn joined us.

"Who's silly?" Thorn asked, removing his dark aviators and tucking them inside his leather jacket.

He really pulled off the badass look. I guess because he actually *was* a badass.

"Lill got bent out of shape when she saw me talking

to Jen's wife one day. She thought I had something going on with her, but I was just talking to her about a security job."

Dex tilted his head, frowning at Lill. "Damn. You're a jealous little thing, aren't you?"

She rolled her eyes. "I never should have told you. Of course you're going to give me major shit about it."

She flipped us the bird and we burst out laughing.

"So, did you tell her the news?" Thorn asked, eyebrows raised.

Lill knit her brow. "News? What news do you guys have?"

She thought she was the only one with news?

I tilted my head at her. "No, ladies first."

Her face brightened like a little kid on Christmas morning.

"I got a call yesterday from Beauté."

Beauté?

"Was that the place you had the job interview?" Thorn asked, taking a draw on his whiskey.

She nodded excitedly. "Yes. Exactly. Well, if you remember, it turned out I'd been talking to them about an internship rather than a real job, which I didn't end up getting anyway." She rolled her eyes.

Oh shit. I remembered now. What a setback that had been.

"But they called me in for a real job interview this Wednesday. It would be a perfect fit. I'd be in charge of all their social media. And if I am disciplined, I can get my romance novels done, too, in the evening." She squeezed her eyes shut and crossed her fingers.

Fuck yeah. She deserved a break, and if those fuckers at Beauté, or whatever the hell it was called, didn't snap up her talent, someone else surely would.

"Well done, baby," Dex said, raising his glass.

She beamed. "It's not a done deal, but it feels good to be considered."

A boost to the confidence was all our girl needed.

"I'm also quitting my writing group. Those people were creeps, anyway. Especially coke dealer Bert and the pervy agent he introduced me to. Fuck them both."

Big things were happening for Lill.

"So what's up with the von Malsens?" she asked.

Funny she should bring that up.

"Just talked to Eckie. He's leaving his post at the UN and heading back to Belgium with Robbie. He wants to start fresh."

Lill drew a long breath. "Wow. Just wow."

"I know right? He's leaving next week, in fact. His assistant is shipping the things he wants from the apartment and getting rid of the rest."

"He's out of here. I feel for the guy. He was cool," Thorn added, shaking his head.

I felt badly for him too. He was a decent man.

"What about Amalia?" Lill asked.

"It sounds like Amalia might have to learn to like prison food," I said.

Lill put her hand over her mouth and shook her head. "So sad. She threw everything away."

"So, that brings us to *our* news," I said, looking at Dex and Thorn.

"What news? That you don't have a job anymore?" Lill asked, laughing.

"Not so fast, baby," Dex said. "We're starting a firm. The three of us. Deverall, Brooks, and Quinton, also known as DBQ."

I had to admit I loved how that sounded. Catchy. Easy to remember. Rolls off the tongue.

And so did Lill. "Oh my god!" she squealed, throwing her arms around Thorn since he was right next to her. "DBQ, that's fucking awesome!"

"We've already got three clients lined up from the von Malsens' building, and Jen's wife is coming to work with us. It will be great to have a woman on the team," Dex added. "But I'm not starting right away," he said, pointing at himself.

"Really?" Lill asked, confused. "Why?"

He beamed. "I'm going back to school at NYU to finish my degree."

Lill's eyes filled with tears. And if I were honest, mine did a bit too. I knew Dex had been haunted for years by his short-lived college career. I'd watched him get kicked out of the university when his scholarship was rescinded, and it was fucking awful. And in spite of all his success in the Army and private sector, and all the money he made and nice things he had, it still hung over his head like a dark cloud.

Money can buy a lot of shit, but not the fulfillment Dex craved.

"And, I'm getting out of my shitty apartment over the bowling alley," Thorn said.

This was perhaps the best news of all. Thorn had come so freaking far.

"I'll stay at Dex's for a while, and then get my own place. Hopefully he won't kick me out before then," he said, high fiving Dex.

"Oh, Thorn, that's so amazing," Lill said, leaning toward him with a big kiss on the cheek.

Thorn raised his eyebrows, clearly wanting more.

"So, I have one last thing to add," Lill said.

"You have more news?" I asked.

She nodded slowly, looking at each of us one by one. "Yup. I do."

We waited. I was sure the guys were wondering the same thing I was.

"What's up, baby?" Thorn asked, taking her hand. "C'mon. Let's have it."

"Well, I'm accepting your offer," she said victoriously.

Holy shit. While this was what I'd hoped for, I'd known to temper my expectations. Not many people could hang with our way of doing things, and the chances of Lill turning us down were always greater than not. We'd been through it before on the rare times we met someone we all liked and wanted to invite to our exclusive little club.

"Well. Aren't you going to say anything?" she asked, laughing.

"That is fucking awesome," Dex hollered, grabbing her hands over the table and kissing them both.

Restrained by the booth where we sat, it was hard to show our excitement. I wanted to pick her up and twirl her around.

And then undress her, of course.

Lill waved at Jen. "Can we get the check, Jen?"

She hadn't figured out yet that drinking at Regulator was free. A perk of *sleeping with the boss*, as Dex had put it.

Jen walked over to our table. "Hey guys. You done?" she asked, gathering our empties.

Lill beamed. "We're not done. We're just starting."

Did you like *Her Dirty Bodyguards*?
Check out *Her Dirty Bartenders*
and
and please leave a review.

GET A FREE SHORT STORY
Join my Insider Group

Exclusive access to private release specials, giveaways, the opportunity to receive advance reader copies (ARCs), and other random musings.

LET'S KEEP IN TOUCH
Mika Lane Newsletter
Email me
Visit me! www.mikalane.com
Friend me! Facebook
Pin me! Pinterest
Follow me! Twitter
Laugh with me! Instagram

ABOUT THE AUTHOR

Dear Reader:

Please join my Insider Group and be the first to hear about giveaways, sales, pre-orders, ARCs, and other cool stuff: http://mikalane.com/join-mailing-list.

Writing has been a passion of mine since, well, forever (my first book was "The Day I Ate the Milkyway," a true fourth-grade masterpiece). These days, steamy romance, both dark and funny, gives purpose to my days and nights as I create worlds and characters who defy the imagination. I live in magical Northern California with my own handsome alpha dude, sometimes known as Mr. Mika Lane, and an evil cat named Bill. These two males also defy my imagination from time to time.

A lover of shiny things, I've been known to try to new recipes on unsuspecting friends, find hiding places so I can read undisturbed, and spend my last dollar on a plane ticket somewhere.

I have a bunch of titles for you to choose from including the perennially favorite Billionaire and Reverse Harem stories. And have you see my Player Series about male escorts who make the ladies of

Hollywood curl their toes and forget their names? Hottttt.... And my Mafia books are are now out in audio.

I'll always promise you a hot, sexy romp with kick-ass but imperfect heroines, and some version of a modern-day happily ever after.

I LOVE to hear from readers when I'm not dreaming up naughty tales to share. Join my Insider Group so we can get to know each other better http://mikalane.com/join-mailing-list, or contact me here: https://mikalane.com/contact.

xoxo
　　Love,
　　Mika

　　　　　　facebook.com/mikalaneauthor
　　　　　　twitter.com/MikaLaneAuthor
　　　　　　instagram.com/mikalaneauthor

Printed in Great Britain
by Amazon